THE MYSTERY MAN

THE NIGHTMARE COLLECTION

Eva Pohler

Eva Pohler Books
20011 Park Ranch
San Antonio, Texas 78259
www.evapohler.com

Publisher's Note: This is a work of fiction. Names, characters, places, and incidents are a product of the author's imagination. Locales and public names are sometimes used for atmospheric purposes. Any resemblance to actual people, living or dead, or to businesses, companies, events, institutions, or locales is completely coincidental.

Book Layout ©2017 BookDesignTemplates.com

Book Cover Design by Najla Qamber Designs

The Mystery Man/ Eva Pohler. -- 1st ed.
Paperback ISBN: 978-1-958390-56-6

Adventure Awaits.
−DEE

Contents

For my family.

First Day

Denise Walker ran in the hot sun across the Trinity University campus from Northrup Hall toward Chapman. The glare from the sun reflecting off the library windows and the metal sculptures and concrete sidewalk made her feel as though the universe had a spotlight on her.

It was hard to believe that, a week ago, she'd held her father's gun to her temple and had come closer to going through with it than she'd ever come before.

When she reached her physics class and peeked inside, she groaned. Unlike the last class, this was an auditorium-style room with over fifty students. There was little chance she wouldn't be noticed. Biting her bottom lip, she slipped through the entrance as inconspicuously as possible to the nearest empty seat. When she looked up, the professor was staring at her.

He continued to stare, first with his eyes wide, and then narrowed, as if he recognized her. She wondered if she'd met him at student orientation or at the convocation, but she was sure she would have remembered him. He was young, attractive, well-built, and tall. His skin was dark, as was his short curly hair. Startling emerald eyes gazed at her from his baffled and beautiful face. How long would he continue to stare?

The blood had rushed to her cheeks, and she looked away, as she picked through her backpack for a notepad and pen.

Once she had unfolded the swivel desktop over her lap and had opened her notepad to the first page, Denise looked up to find the professor was still staring at her. She glanced around the room. Other students were now looking at her, too.

"I'm sorry I'm late, Professor Nadir," Denise said as she nervously twirled a strand of her black hair around her index finger. "I went to room 124 in Northrup Hall by accident and didn't realize I was in the wrong classroom until after the teacher had taken attendance."

The professor surprised her with a grin. He had an adorable face when he smiled, and this relaxed her. He muttered something beneath his breath—she wished she could hear it. Then he said, "That's perfectly fine, Dee—er, Denise."

What the heck? How did he already know her by name in a class of over fifty students?

"As I was saying," the professor said. "If you bought your textbook, return it. Get your money back. Everything in it is outdated." He paused and glanced at the students and then found Denise again. "What I'm about to teach you in this course will blow your mind."

Denise looked away, embarrassed again by his attention, and scratched out a note on her notepad: *Blow my mind.*

"The very first lesson I want you all to understand is this: Contrary to Einstein's theory, it *is* possible for an object to travel faster than the speed of light. It only appears to be otherwise, because the object traveling at this speed is *without* light, and therefore, *invisible.*"

Denise couldn't stop herself from raising a hand.

Professor Nadir laughed. Why would he laugh? But she kept her hand raised until he called her by name.

"If the object is invisible, how can your statement be proven?" she asked.

"Aha!" he said, smiling wider and lifting a finger in the air. "I'm glad you asked. That will be the topic of our first unit. Before tomorrow, I want you to read everything you can find on Einstein's theory of relativity. I'm releasing you early today, but don't get used to it. See you next time."

Denise glanced around at the other students gathering their backpacks and purses and folding their desks before making their way down the rows and out of the room. Brian Jameson stood at the top of the steps near one of the back exits. Brian Jameson? She hadn't noticed him among the crowd of students, and now her heart skipped a beat. His body had filled out—was more muscular than it had been in high school. His brown hair had grown out into wavy locks that fell to his ears. She waved at him and then turned away, down the steps toward the professor.

As Professor Nadir was packing his leather satchel, he didn't see her coming toward him. She cleared her throat. When he looked up at her, a huge smile crossed his face. It was perplexing and breathtaking.

"I want to apologize again for being late," she managed to say, despite how captivated she was by the man standing in front of her. "I was hoping to make a better impression on the first day."

"You have nothing to fear." He winked. "Consider me greatly impressed."

A chuckle escaped from her throat as blood rushed to her cheeks. "That hardly seems possible." She wondered if he was teasing her. "However, I'm very impressed by how quickly you learn your students' names."

Through his chocolate complexion came the pinkish hue of his own blush. "I'm not good with names. I called attendance, and it was only by the power of deduction that I came to know yours."

This was getting awkward. "I was the only student missing out of fifty or sixty?"

"Seventy-two. And there were seven missing, but you were the only female."

She felt relieved and gave him a nod of understanding. The tension left her body as she was reassured that nothing out of the ordinary was going on between them.

He swept up his book satchel and headed toward the front exit. "I'll see you on Wednesday, Denise."

"Have a good day, Professor," she said.

A whirlwind of heat washed over her as she watched him leave.

"Denise!"

She glanced up to the exit at the back of the room where Brian was waiting. So, he'd waited for her. As she raced up the steps, two at a time, she wondered what on earth he could possibly have to say to her. She met him on the landing, where he was holding the door open.

"That was strange," he said.

"I know. Right?" She stepped into the hallway, where others were headed to lecture halls and classrooms. "Long-time, no-see. How've you been?"

"Not as good as I am now," he said with a cheesy smile. "Are you going to another class?"

"Composition. You?"

"Calculus."

"How fun." Brian knew her well enough to know she wasn't being sarcastic. They both loved math.

"And after that?" he asked, as they rounded the corner of the hall-way.

"I have a break, for lunch."

"Want to meet up at Earl Abel's? Around eleven-thirty?"

She smiled up at him. "Okay. Yeah. Sure."

As they parted ways in front of her next classroom, she felt a tingle work down her spine. Brian was interested in her again, and she wasn't sure how she felt about it.

Earl Abel's was bustling with lunchtime diners and with the aromas of chicken, potatoes, and pie when Denise arrived and cased the entrance for Brian. When she didn't spot him, she stood with a crowd of others near the hostess station feeling unsure about her decision to lunch with him. Things had ended awkwardly between them in high school. Then she'd taken two years off to save money, and he'd gone on ahead of her to Trinity. They were the same age, but he must be a junior by now, and he hadn't so much as given her a text or a phone call in the two years since they'd last seen one another. Did he really think they could pick up where they'd left off?

The hostess, not much younger than she, asked for her name.

"Denise, party of two."

"I'll get you seated in about ten minutes," the hostess said.

"Thanks."

Maybe it *wasn't* Brian's intention to pick up where things were before, she scolded herself. They could be friends, couldn't they? This was just a lunch, not a romantic riverboat cruise or a sunset at Enchanted Rock. She closed her eyes as the wave of memories with Brian accosted her.

"Are you okay?"

She opened her eyes to see Brian looking down at her.

"Yeah. Fine. How was your calculus class?"

"Great. I have the same teacher I had last semester, for Calc Two. She knows her stuff. How was Composition?"

"The jury's still out on that." She lifted her brows and grimaced. "We shall see."

After a few more minutes of small talk, the hostess took them to their table, and they ordered. Their food arrived, and they continued to chat. As Brian told her a little more about his major (math), his job (teaching assistant in the math department), and his aspirations (a professorship at a university after grad school), she continued to assess his intentions toward her. There was something about the way he gazed into her eyes that gave her the feeling he wanted to be more than friends.

She still didn't know how she felt about that.

When the check came, he offered to pay, but wouldn't that make it a date? Since she still wasn't sure what she wanted, she insisted on paying her share of the bill. Afterward, he walked her to her car and kissed her softly on the cheek.

"See you in Physics on Wednesday," he said in that low, gentle voice that used to send chills of pleasure down her body.

There may have been a few chills today.

"See you then, Brian."

That evening after her school day was over, Denise made a pot of beef stew and studied while it cooked. She did her calculus, biology, and composition homework first. Then, after she added the veggies to the stew, she sat at the kitchen table with her laptop and scoured the internet for all things related to Einstein's theories.

Only one article challenged the theory that nothing could surpass the speed of light, and it was written by Professor Nadir. Did the university know he was teaching students to disregard mainstream theories so that he could tout his own? She reached into her backpack and took out the heavy textbook, which the professor had said to return. Surely there was something valuable here. Denise wondered if she should drop Nadir's course and try to get into another. She was serious about her education and didn't want to waste time learning from some on-the-fringe scientist who could turn out to be a crackpot—especially one who distracted her with his amazing looks and intense eyes.

She decided to Google her professor. The results page was full of links:

"Chemotherapy Becomes a Thing of the Past, Thanks to Dr. Nadir," "Increased Brain Function with Light Therapy, by Markos Nadir,"

"Measuring Objects that Surpass the Speed of Light," and "The Future with Time Travel" were among them. Denise clicked on a few of the links and skimmed to see if they were about her professor. Every one of them referred to Markos Nadir as a Harvard professor. Was this a different man? She clicked on the Trinity University website and looked up his biography. There was that incredible face staring back at her again. According to his bio, he'd recently left Harvard to teach at Trinity. This was his first year.

Her curiosity was piqued. Why had he come to Trinity? And why had he reacted to her in his classroom as though he knew her?

When the stew was ready, she filled two bowls and carried them on a tray, along with glasses of iced tea, to her father's room.

His old console television was on, playing softly from on top of his antique chest of drawers, but he wasn't watching it. He was sitting in bed, staring at nothing.

"Hey, Daddy." Denise set the tray down on the bedside table and fell into her chair next to him. "Ready for some supper?"

"Mmm. Yes, Baby. Smells good. What is it?"

She handed him a bowl. "Beef stew. Does that sound good?"

"It sure does. Thank you."

"It's hot, so be careful."

She watched him blow on a spoonful. It always reminded her of the days when he blew on her food when she was a little girl. He puckered his thick lips, like a flautist. His long lashes shielded his dark brown eyes and touched his dark, hallow cheeks. His chin, covered in a salt and pepper scruffy beard, moved ever-so-slightly as he leaned closer to the spoon and slurped up the stew.

"Is it good?" she asked.

"Delicious, as always. Thank you, Baby."

No matter how thin he became, he always had a twinkle in his eyes for her.

"You're welcome, Daddy." She ate a bite. It was good. Each batch got better and better.

"How was your first day of school?" he asked.

"Interesting," she said.

"Why do I get the feeling that 'interesting' isn't a good thing?"

She told him what had happened in her physics class with Professor Nadir.

"Sounds like your professor was flirting with you," her father said.

"Daddy!"

"You don't seem to realize how beautiful you are—the spitting image of your mother."

"I'm more black than white. I take after you." Denise twirled a strand of her hair, coarse like her fathers, around her index finger.

"You have her bone structure and her almond-shaped eyes."

"Brown, like yours."

"True."

"I guess that makes me the perfect combination of you both."

"That it does! So, you better get used to all the attention you're going to get in college, from both the teachers and the students."

"Oh, Daddy. You're just biased."

"But not blind. Not yet, anyway."

She told him what Professor Nadir had said about invisible objects traveling faster than the speed of light.

"Now that right there sounds fascinating. Maybe you should invite him over for supper some time, so I can hear what he has to say."

"Oh, Daddy! I'm not going to invite my professor over for supper! That's not what people do!"

"Hmmm. We'll see about that."

The next morning, Denise sat in her chair in the room she rented at the salon, braiding extensions into her client's hair. The client, Lucinda, an old high school friend, sat on a bean bag on the floor between Denise's legs, watching Netflix on Denise's laptop. Netflix helped pass the time for her and her clients on Tuesdays and Thursdays (and sometimes on Saturdays), and it was the only chance Denise ever had to watch any shows.

When the final episode of their show ended, they dried their eyes, and Denise asked, "Now what do you want to watch?"

"I don't know," Lucinda said. "Maybe I need a break. I just want to sit here and close my eyes."

Denise thought she could use a little quiet time, too, so she braided in silence while her thoughts went back to the previous day—first to Brian, and then to Professor Nadir, who had visited her last night in her dreams.

It hadn't been an erotic dream, but it had come close and had been full of enough sexual tension to make her want to return to the dream as soon as she'd awakened.

Her thoughts were interrupted when Lucinda said, "Brian Jameson just tweeted that he had lunch with you yesterday." Lucinda turned to see Denise's face—for evidence, Denise supposed.

Denise couldn't suppress the smile. "It was just lunch, jeez."

"That's exactly how it started last time!" Lucinda laughed.

Denise pulled on Lucinda's hair. "Hold still."

"You can't change the subject. How was it?"

"The food was good."

"You know that's not what I mean."

"Brian's nice, smart, hot…"

"Don't you know it, girlfriend."

Denise frowned. "But I'm not sure I want to go there again."

"You were together our entire senior year, weren't you?" Lucinda asked.

"Yep."

"What happened?"

Denise shrugged, even though Lucinda couldn't see her. "I really don't know."

Second Week

Denise decided not to arrive early to her physics class on the following Monday, because when she'd done so the previous Wednesday and Friday, Brian had taken one of the empty seats beside her and had whispered to her throughout the lecture. He'd been funny and charming, as ever, but Denise didn't want to miss a single word Professor Nadir had to say. She'd become extremely interested in his discussion of space-time.

She walked through one of the back entrances at the top of the room with only a minute to spare. Brian waved from their usual seats—he'd saved hers. She waved back but indicated she was going to slip into one of the seats in back. He stood up, as if he would join her, but before he got very far, the professor began his lecture. Denise sighed with relief when Brian decided to stay put.

Denise's feelings of relief were quickly replaced with anxiety when Professor Nadir scoured the room for her face. She knew, before his eyes met hers, that he was searching for her. She wasn't sure how she knew it, but when his gaze fell on her, and he smiled and gave her a nod, she slid down in her seat, wishing to avoid the glances of the other students, who noticed.

Why did the professor seem to have taken an interest in her?

"Last time we discussed the nature of black holes," the professor began, "and how Einstein theorized they impacted space-time. We discussed gravitational lensing. Can anyone recall a good example of this?"

Several students raised their hands, and the one called on replied, "Einstein's Cross—a quasar in the Pegasus constellation."

"Yes," the professor said. "Thank you. You are probably wondering by now what black holes have to do with my claim that some objects are capable of moving faster than the speed of light. Well, let me explain. A black hole is a dense, dark mass that can only be detected by its impact on its environment. It's absent of light, yes?"

Denise and many other students nodded.

"It is the same with objects traveling faster than light," he explained. "They leave behind a shimmering effect."

Denise wrote *shimmering effect* on her notepad.

"From a distance, a fast-moving baseball appears smaller than one lobbed slowly up into the air, right?" the professor asked. "But the fast-moving baseball has greater mass than the slow-moving one, because the faster something moves, the greater its kinetic energy and, thus, its mass. Energy and mass are essentially two manifestations of the same thing. Do you follow me so far?"

Denise thought so.

"This increase in mass for the fast-moving object is the reason Einstein concluded that no object could travel faster than light," the professor continued. "He postulated that mass becomes infinite when it reaches light speed."

"But it doesn't?" Denise asked, before she realized the question had escaped her throat.

"No," he replied with a smile.

Brian glanced back at her and grinned.

"Everything is relative in the universe," the professor said. "Except the speed of light. It's the one constant."

Denise wrote, *The speed of light is the only constant in the universe.*

"And I don't believe dark objects travel faster than the speed of light in nature," the professor said. "At least, I have not seen any evidence of this. However, people are capable of manipulating objects through space-time beyond light speed. I have seen this with my own eyes. The shimmering effect."

Denise underlined *shimmering effect* in her notes.

As the professor spoke more about gravitational lensing and waving and the shimmering effect, Denise hung on his every word. She was one hundred percent absorbed and fascinated by the subject. She could hardly believe it when the class came to an end.

"Before I dismiss you, I want to remind you of something I have stated at the close of each class period. Can anyone guess it?"

A student raised his hand and said, "Time does not pass at the same rate for everyone. Time isn't constant."

"Precisely," the professor said. "I'll see you on Wednesday."

Denise raised her hand. "Wait, Professor?"

Markos Nadir smiled up at her. "Yes, Denise?"

"If time isn't constant…"

"Uh-huh?"

"And if light is measured in light-*years*…" she continued.

"A light-year is a unit of *distance*," he replied. "Not of *time*."

"But it's based on the amount of distance light travels in a year, and years are units of time."

"Very good, Denise," he said. "I knew you would be brilliant."

She lifted her brows as heat rushed to her face. What was that supposed to mean?

"As inhabitants of this planet," the professor continued, "we share the same frame of reference for what defines a year; thus, from our point of view, it remains constant."

The other students were showing signs of frustration and eagerness to leave the classroom—the professor had, after all, already ended class, and Denise was keeping them with her questions.

"Thank you, Professor," she said.

"The pleasure is mine. I'll see you all next time."

Brian caught up with her near the back exit and gave her a sheepish grin. "How's it going?"

"Good." She led him from the lecture hall, navigating through the crowd of other students.

"Did you do anything this weekend?" he asked, as he followed her through the hall.

"Just studied. You?"

"Same." Then he added, "So I was thinking maybe this weekend, we could, I don't know, do something."

Denise's throat tightened. She really wasn't sure she wanted to do this again. Everything about Brian still felt…unresolved. But, so as not to appear rude, she asked, "Like what?"

"Maybe dinner and a movie?"

So, he was definitely interested, and he was asking her out on a real date this time. Lunch was one thing. But dinner and a movie?

Before she could reply, he said, "Think about it, and I'll catch up with you later."

Friday night, after the movie, as she and Brian sat across from one another in a quiet corner booth at Olive Garden, Brian said, "So, why didn't you ever reply to my letter?"

She had just taken a bite of her ravioli, and it nearly fell from her mouth when her jaw dropped open. After she swallowed the bite, she asked, "What letter?"

He arched a brow. "What do you mean, 'what letter'? I poured my heart and soul out in that thing. You know what letter."

"No, I don't." Her heart seemed to stand still. "What did it say?"

"What? You never got it?"

She shook her head.

"Well, that explains a lot."

"Brian, what are you talking about?"

"I thought the reason we haven't spoken in the last two years had something to do with what I wrote in the letter," he explained.

Denise dropped her fork on her plate and was now numb and unable to eat. "What did the letter say?"

"That I adored you and wanted to spend my life with you."

Denise covered her mouth and stared at him in shock for nearly a full minute. "I don't know what to say. I had no idea."

"So why did you stop talking to me?" he asked.

"You stopped talking to me," she insisted. "You didn't return any of my texts or calls."

"You called me?"

"A gazillion times. I thought you were in an accident. I heard from a friend that you were okay. And then I saw you on Twitter and Facebook and figured you…"

"Oh, no," he said. "I dropped my phone." He snapped his fingers. "I couldn't get any of my contacts. I kept thinking you'd come by, like you always did."

His parents were never home, so they'd tended to hang out there more than they had at her house.

"Why didn't you come to my house?" she asked. "Or email me, or reach out to me on Twitter or Facebook?"

"I thought you read my letter and didn't feel the same way. I was scared."

"I wouldn't just stop talking to you," she said. "I'd never do something like that."

He looked down at his plate.

Denise wasn't sure how she felt about this news. Brian had written her a letter confessing his feelings for her and then had assumed she didn't reciprocate. *This* was what had happened? She was confused.

"I need a drink," he said suddenly.

"You want a glass of wine?"

"No, not here. It's too expensive. Why don't we go to Crazy Chuck's?"

Denise frowned. It was a club. She wasn't sure she was up for it, but Brian looked like he really wanted to go, and she felt bad for how things had ended.

"Alright," she finally said. "But I'm not twenty-one."

"Oh, that's right. Never mind, then."

"It's okay."

"Sure?"

She nodded.

They were quiet during the drive. Denise was still trying to process what Brian had said about the letter. He'd wanted to spend the rest of his life with her, and, when she hadn't come over, he'd assumed the letter had freaked her out. This changed everything.

She glanced sideways at him. But if he really had felt that way, he should have come to see her—or, he could have gotten her number from a mutual friend. He shouldn't have given up so easily. Maybe he was too young. Maybe if it had happened now, he would have tried harder and not run away.

Or maybe he was making the whole thing up, and there was no letter. She glanced at him again. Was he capable of being that deceptive?

Once inside the club, Brian left her standing near the dance floor to get their drinks. She was glad to have a little time away from him to think. She tried to remember all that had happened in the weeks when he hadn't returned any of her texts or calls.

The club was crowded with both college-aged students and people in their thirties. Men—young and older—stood along the perimeter of the dance floor near the two bars sipping drinks and watching the dancers— mostly women—perform a line dance. Some of them were boisterous and really into the dance moves, and others were tentative, still learning. Denise enjoyed this distraction from her confused feelings.

Suddenly a woman, tall and white, was beside her. Even her blouse and miniskirt were white. The only hint of color on the woman—about mid-twenties, Denise guessed—was the blue in her eyes.

"You see Hex, over there?" the woman said to Denise.

Denise followed the woman's gaze across the room, where a tall and older black man with rings on his fingers and one gold tooth smiled back at her before looking away. He was a hunk of a man—with more muscles than she'd ever seen up-close and personal. He was sexy in a bad way.

"Yeah?" Denise replied.

"He's not an easy catch—smart, wealthy. I've been trying to get him to fall in love with me for years."

"Maybe you should move on."

"Maybe I should." The woman laughed. "Well, he's into you, any-way."

Denise glanced at Hex again. He wasn't looking at her—was watch-ing the dancers.

"I'm here with someone," Denise explained. "Excuse me."

She made her escape and sought Brian. He was still waiting in line to buy their drinks. She caught up to him and told him she was going to the ladies' room and would meet up with him after.

The line for the stalls in the bathroom was even longer than the one at the bar. Denise wished they hadn't come. She was tired and needed to pee.

She left the line in the ladies' room to return to the bar where Brian was waiting in line and was shocked to see another girl's arms wrapped around his neck. She watched them for a few moments, hoping to give Brian a chance. Maybe the other girl was coming on to him, and he was attempting to let her down easy.

But that's not what she saw. Brian leaned in and kissed the girl on the lips, then he whispered something in her ear before she nodded, smiling, as she turned to leave.

Denise had no time for this kind of nonsense in her life. If Brian didn't know what he wanted, then she didn't want to have anything to do with him. How dare he kiss another girl while on a date with her? What nerve? And what stupidity? Now things would be awkward in class for the rest of the semester.

Denise decided she would call a cab. She searched one up on her phone.

She avoided glancing in Brian's direction as she made her way through the crowd toward the exit. Before she reached it, the white girl caught up to her and said, "Hex wants to talk to you. Interested?"

Denise hesitated. She wouldn't mind using this opportunity to get back at Brian. Besides, what harm could there be in talking to the man?

"Where is he?" Denise asked.

"Outside, in the parking lot."

"I was just about to call a cab. If he wants to wait with me out front, I'll talk to him."

"You got it," the girl said. "He'll meet you there in a few."

Denise watched the white girl leave through the exit on her high stilettos, hips swinging. If that girl was so interested in Hex, why was she setting him up with Denise? She must not think very highly of herself.

Denise stepped out beneath the awning, where one of the club bouncers stood checking IDs. She took a few steps into the parking lot to get away from the line at the door. She had another shock when Professor Nadir approached her.

"You need to get out of here," he said. "Come with me, and I'll take you home."

"Professor Nadir? What are you doing here?"

He looked incredible in jeans and t-shirt.

"Saving you. Now come on."

Denise refused to follow him. "Saving me? From what?"

Markos Nadir moved nearer and whispered, "The woman in white and the man called Hex are setting you up."

His breath sent chills of pleasure across her skin, but she pulled back and studied his face. How did he know she'd been talking to the white woman?

"I've seen it before, at another club. I'm surprised they haven't been caught by now. Anyway, I noticed the girl talking to you and was worried you'd fall into their trap."

"I didn't see you inside."

"I haven't been in yet. I just arrived."

"I don't know what to say."

"Come with me. Or, at least, let me call you a cab."

She looked at her phone, which still displayed her search results for "taxi." Not wanting to wait around for Hex, the white girl, or Brian to come looking for her, she decided to go with Professor Nadir.

Besides, he was superhot in his faded jeans and snug t-shirt. Being alone with him made her hyper-aware of his every move, his every muscle. She liked that feeling.

In the car, she said, "Did you come alone or with friends?"

"Alone. I'm not from here."

"That's right. You're from Cambridge."

He gave her a surprised glance. "You looked me up."

"I was curious about you."

"Well, I'm not originally from Cambridge, either."

"Oh? Where are you from?"

He gave her another glance. "I was born in New York City, but that's not exactly where I'm from. You won't have heard of it."

She had a feeling he didn't want to talk about it, so she left it at that. "Where are we going?"

"To your house. I'll drop you off." Then he quickly added, "Which direction?"

"You're going the right way. I'll tell you when you need to exit."

She had a strange feeling that he already knew where to go.

When they reached her house, he pulled up beside the curb and stopped the car. "Listen, Denise. You're a smart girl, and I don't mean to meddle, but that Brian kid is not for you. And you should avoid talking to strange men at clubs. That's how women get hurt."

She was startled by his direct approach. What had felt like a sweet gesture by a knight in shining armor had quickly become a lecture from a righteous, judgmental dick.

"It sounds like you do mean to meddle, Professor." She opened the car door.

"I'm only trying to help."

"Thanks for the ride." She stepped out, onto the sidewalk.

"I'll see you in class."

She met his eyes once more before closing the car door and turning up the sidewalk to her house.

Her father was still awake, as usual, when she looked in on him. He didn't sleep much anymore—maybe four or five hours each night.

"Hi, Daddy," she said. "What are you watching?"

"Oh, hello, Baby. The History Channel. Nothing I haven't seen before. It's interesting, though. Did you have a good time with Brian?"

"Not really. I'm done with him, Daddy."

"Good. 'Cause I never liked him anyway."

They both laughed.

"I'm going to bed," she said. "Good night."

"Good night, Baby."

After she changed and crawled beneath her covers, Denise found herself thinking less about Brian and more about Markos Nadir.

CHAPTER THREE

Third Month

In late October, Denise arrived early Wednesday to her physics class to get herself mentally prepared for the mid-term. It was an essay exam, and she had spent the last few weeks studying for it. She silently cursed when Brian sat down in the desk beside her in the back of the lecture hall. After their date, she'd told him what she'd seen at the bar. He'd made some lame excuse she hadn't believed, and she'd told him she wasn't interested in him. If she was to be honest with herself, she was over him a long time ago.

For the last two months, they'd barely spoken, avoiding each other in the classroom. She'd arrive late and sit in the back, and, as soon as class was over, she'd rush off to Composition.

"Hey," he said now without looking at her.

"Hey." She had nothing more to say and really wished he'd move to another desk.

"Look, I'm sorry," he said. "I should have told Chastity that I was at the club with you. I lied to you, and I lied to her."

"Can we not talk about this right now?" She glanced around at the other students. Only a few had arrived, as the class wouldn't start for another fifteen minutes.

"I don't know what's wrong with me," he said. "Every time I get close to a girl, I run away and hide. First you. Then Chastity."

"Not now, Brian," she insisted. "I'm trying to stay focused for the test."

"Just tell me you forgive me, and I'll leave you alone."

"I forgive you. But I'd appreciate it if you gave me some space."

"Thanks. No problem." He got up and moved a few seats away.

Now she was frazzled and angry. Her concentration and focus were gone. Tears welled in her eyes. She'd studied so hard, and she really wanted an A in the class. More importantly, she wanted to impress her professor.

Ever since he'd "rescued" her from Hex and the white girl, Denise hadn't stopped thinking of Markos Nadir. She imagined kissing him and wondered what it would feel like to be in his arms. She berated herself for thinking of him that way, but she hadn't been able to stop. There was something about him. She could tell he felt the same way about her.

As soon as the professor entered the lecture hall, she felt her body respond. Her anxiety over the test, her anger over Brian, and her growing feelings for Professor Nadir had conspired against her, making her nauseated and weak. Her hands trembled. Would she be able to write her essay? She blinked and bit her lip, hoping she wouldn't faint.

Without fail, Professor Nadir searched the seats in the auditorium-style lecture hall until his green eyes settled on her. It made her heart skip a beat every time. He was more aware of her than he was of any other student in the room. It both frightened and exhilarated her.

He cleared his throat and gave a few instructions, reminding the students that they could turn in their exams and leave as soon as they were finished. There was no need to stay until the very end of the period.

Denise had a feeling she would need every second of the fifty-minute class. Her stomach churned as the professor handed out the exams, asking the person on the aisle seat of each row to take one and pass the exams down to the rest of the students. When Professor Nadir finally reached the last row of desks and handed her the exams, she smiled up at him, her lips twitching. Her teeth threatened to chatter, so she shut her mouth and took her exam before passing the others to the person beside her. She fought the urge to watch Markos Nadir retreat from the top of the lecture hall down to the podium at the front of the room.

With trembling hands, she read the essay question: *Given what we've discussed about space-time, do you believe time travel is possible? Please explain and defend your answer.*

This was not what she had expected. What about Newtonian mechanics, fluid mechanics and thermal physics, electricity and magnetism, and waves and optics—all things she had killed herself memorizing for the exam? The only subjects relevant to a discussion of time-travel were their units on gravitational waving and traversing wormholes. She looked around the room to see if any of the other students were as worried as she, but everyone else leaned over their paper and had already begun to write.

Denise skipped the rest of her classes on Wednesday and canceled all her hair appointments for Thursday because she was sick to her stomach. Her father said maybe she had food poisoning. At first, she thought so, too, but, after a day of vomiting, she still felt crummy. On Friday, she stayed home again and laid in bed, miserable. She only got up to pee and to heat something up for her father to eat.

On Friday afternoon, she was worried when she received a call from a university phone number and taken aback when she answered it only to discover it was Professor Nadir calling her personal cell phone.

"Denise? I'm sorry to disturb you, but it is imperative that you hear the lecture I gave to the rest of the students before Monday, as I laid the foundation for Monday's lecture today. Where were you? Are you ill?"

"Yes, Professor. I'm not feeling well." She wrinkled her nose, wondering what the heck. Was he calling every student who'd been absent today?

"Can you come by my office tomorrow, assuming you feel better? I want to go over what you missed."

"Um. Do you really think that's necessary?" she asked. "I was going to work tomorrow, if I'm up to it."

Despite her reply, she was exhilarated by the idea of spending time with him.

"It's absolutely necessary. What about Sunday?"

"Will you be meeting with all the students who missed today's lecture?" she asked suspiciously. Could he really feel for her what she was feeling for him?

"Only you. You're my brightest pupil."

She clutched her stomach. "Wait 'til you read my exam."

"I have. It was brilliant."

Denise perked up. "Seriously? But I argued in favor of time travel! Afterward, I was sick, literally sick, because, scientifically, it really is a stretch, and I can't believe it. I can argue in favor of it, but I just can't make the leap intellectually."

"Your essay was not a disappointment. Quite the opposite. But if you don't catch up before Monday, you'll be behind and missing crucial information for the second half of the course. I'll be in my office all weekend. Please call me when you're on your way."

The professor hung up before Denise could say more.

Saturday, Denise felt much better. Just knowing that her professor had liked her essay relieved her nausea and other symptoms. Her father told her it was probably stress that had made her so ill. She wouldn't have agreed if not for the immediate relief she felt after speaking with Markos Nadir.

She called the professor Saturday evening when she was finished with the clients she had rescheduled from Thursday. Professor Nadir wanted her to come to his office immediately, but she needed to cook for her father, so she scheduled an appointment for Sunday morning at nine o'clock. That would still give her time to get home to make her father's favorite Sunday dinner. It was the one day of the week that he came out of his room and ate with her at the table. At least once a month, they even invited her older brother, Girard, and his wife, Kassia, and Aunt Latisha—her father's sister—over to join them, which they had done for tomorrow, and Denise was looking forward to seeing them. The Sunday meal had been a habit formed by Denise's mother, and her father had kept it, no matter how poorly he felt.

Sunday morning, Denise was nervous as she knocked on Professor Nadir's office door. The rest of the building was quiet. It seemed he was the only member of the faculty there today.

He called out for her to come in.

Her heart raced as she opened the door. He sat behind his desk, in front of the office window, facing her. He wore a snug-fitting baby blue polo shirt and faded jeans. His emerald eyes gazed up at her from his dark, chiseled face. The light from the window behind him accentuated his beautiful form.

She looked away from his eyes to catch her breath, pretending to be interested in the objects filling the room.

A stack of books took up one corner of his desk. A bookcase took up the right wall, and another window and two club chairs were on the left. The office was immaculate—tidier than she kept her father's house. And there were interesting futuristic knickknacks and gadgets on the bookcase and on a sideboard and file cabinet flanking the seating area.

"Please, have a seat," he said, bringing her from her reverie.

"I like your office," she said as she sat in the chair nearest his desk. "What's that?"

She pointed to a round device sitting on the end table between the two club chairs. The device had colored lights shooting from its center, imposing rays of color on the ceiling and walls.

"It's called a quantum compass. It's just a model. Hasn't been invented yet." He cleared his throat.

She next noticed a framed photo, which faced the professor on the corner of his desk nearest her. She was shocked by how much the woman in the photo resembled her.

"That woman," Denise said, pointing to the photo. "Who is she?"

"Mariela, my late wife."

Denise felt the blood leave her face. "Oh, I'm so sorry."

"It's okay. Thank you."

"Mariela? Such a pretty name. My brother and his wife are having a girl later this month, and they're planning to call *her* Mariela."

"What a coincidence," he said, looking away, his long lashes caressing his cheek bones and guarding his stunning eyes.

"I only asked about the photo because, well, I couldn't help but notice how much she looks like me." Denise laughed nervously.

"Believe me," he said, still avoiding her eyes. "Your resemblance to her has not gone unnoticed."

Now she felt awkward and uncomfortable, but simultaneously enthralled. Was that why he seemed to like her so much? She reminded him of his wife? A chill moved down her back, and she fidgeted in the chair. "How long ago did she pass?"

He sucked in his lips and looked up, at the ceiling. "I'm afraid that's difficult for me to talk about."

Blood rushed to her cheeks. "I'm sorry. I didn't mean to pry."

"No, I'm the one who's sorry," he finally met her eyes, and her heart skipped a beat. "I didn't mean to make you feel uneasy."

She smiled. "It's okay, Professor."

"Please, call me Markos." He rested an ankle on his opposite knee and sat back in his chair, more relaxed. "It sounds so strange to hear you call me 'Professor.'"

She cocked her head to the side. That made no sense whatsoever. "Okay, Markos." It felt good to say his first name. It was more intimate. "What did I miss on Friday?"

He gave her a piece of paper with notes typed on it and moved his desk chair closer to her. "I handed this out to the class and went over it. I'd like to go over it now with you, if you have time. It should take us about thirty minutes."

"Of course," she said, feeling jittery with him so close. "That's why I'm here."

"You see the first point? The Alcubierre Warp Drive?"

Denise nodded.

"This explains a manipulation of space-time fabric with the use of a drive, or a vacuum, that will contract the space in front of a vessel and expand it behind. This would enable a craft to travel faster than light."

"Like warp speed in *Star Trek*?"

Markos Nadir laughed. "Yes. Exactly. It requires negative mass, or exotic matter."

"How interesting."

"And the second point is one we've already discussed—the presence of wormholes and how traversing them can result in time travel."

"Right. That's what I based most of my essay on."

"That concept was *also* featured in *Star Trek*," Markos pointed out.

"Oh, yeah. The movie from a few years ago, right? When Spock from the future travels through a wormhole to the past and meets his younger self?"

"That's the one. It's a classic."

Although it was hardly old enough to be called a classic, in her opinion, she beamed up at him and said, "I loved it."

Markos met her eyes and studied her lips, which Denise couldn't prevent from trembling slightly. Then he cleared his throat. "Yes. Now look at the next point, about the closed time-like curves, by Godel."

"Okay. What's that about?"

"If the fabric of space-time is curved, like our universe and galaxy—due to gravity—a vessel could curve back on its past."

"You mean travel back in time?"

"Exactly."

"But how could a vessel curve back? By accident?"

"It *can* occur by accident," he said with a smile. "But it can also be manipulated to occur."

"How?"

"By creating enough gravitational energy to bend the fabric of space-time," he replied. "One problem is that once the vessel is propelled back, it will create a loop."

"A loop?"

"Think of time as a straight line. All the points along this line exist simultaneously on this line, and, as we move through space, we experience time. Are you with me so far?"

Denise nodded.

"Now imagine the closed time-like curve bending back that line at one point, creating a loop." He drew a picture that looked like a roller-coaster ride called the Boomerang. "The straight line of time continues past the loop, and only the time-traveler and his vessel has taken this loop back on the timeline. But his younger self continues to exist back here on the timeline, right? And as the time traveler moves forward through space, he now occupies the same space as his younger self. You see?"

Denise nodded.

"But if, as he's experiencing the line for the second time, his younger self doesn't take that same loop back in time, the traveler won't exist on any of these points. The timeline will have been altered. If his younger self never goes back, then there is no time-traveler on any point of the timeline."

"How interesting." Denise was enthralled with the concept, and, full of excitement, leaned toward the professor. "Do you think it's possible that we could actually bend the fabric of space-time to travel to the past?"

"Yes. I do. It will take an enormous amount of energy, but I do believe it will happen."

"It's fascinating to think about."

The professor's emerald eyes beamed back at her. "I'm glad you think so. I thought you might."

"I'm so glad I decided not to drop your class."

Markos narrowed his eyes. "You considered it?"

"When you told us to ditch our textbooks, yes." She smiled sheepishly.

He laughed. "I suppose that was rather unorthodox, but hopefully it will soon make sense to you."

He stood up, so she stood, too, and said, "Thank you so much, Professor—I mean, Markos. I'm totally excited now."

He put a hand on her shoulder. "It's my pleasure, Denise. Thanks for coming by."

She looked up at him, standing so close, his hand touching her bare skin. She felt a jolt of electricity pass through his fingers and down her arm.

He pulled his hand away, blushing, and, looking down at the carpet, he said, "Have a nice day."

Awkwardly, she turned and crossed the room to the door. "You, too. And thanks again."

"And Denise?" he called as she opened the door to leave.

"Yes?"

"I really enjoyed our conversation."

"I did, too."

"Would you like to meet for coffee sometime?"

She bit her lip to keep her jaw from dropping open. "Um, yes. I would. Very much."

"I can't tomorrow, but how about Wednesday morning, before class?"

"That should work."

"There's a Starbucks off campus on Hildebrand."

"Sure. What time?"

"Would eight o'clock be too early?"

She wanted to say that there was no time too early for him, but, instead, she smiled and said. "Not at all. See you then."

"But you'll be in class tomorrow, won't you?"

She felt silly and smiled sheepishly again. "Yes. I will. See you tomorrow."

She rushed from his office before she made more of a fool of herself.

Monday came early for Denise because she'd been up until three in the morning. During their Sunday dinner, her brother's wife, Kassia, had gone into labor, and little Mariela had been born at two in the morning on October twentieth. Her father had waited up for Denise to return from the hospital, and she had shown him pictures on her phone of his first grandbaby. It had brought tears to both of their eyes—both happy and sad. They were happy to welcome a sweet new member to their family, but they were sad that Denise's mother couldn't have been there to meet her, too.

As sleepy as she was when her alarm went off a few hours later, Denise forced herself out of bed. Markos had gone to too much trouble to prepare her for today's lecture for her to miss it.

She felt the jolt of electricity that came every time he sought her in the lecture hall. When their eyes met, he smiled and looked away, clearing his throat. Then he began. At first, Denise could only study the man—the way he filled out his clothes, his mesmerizing emerald eyes, and his soothing voice. But eventually, and much to her surprise, she was soon captivated by *what* he was saying as much as she was by *how* he was saying it.

After class, he called her down to his podium. She had to skirt awkwardly past Brian in the aisle before she could make her way down the steps to Markos.

"Did you have any questions about what I covered today?" he asked her. "It's very important that you understand the principles of closed time-like curves."

"No questions. I totally get it."

"Good." Then he asked, "Are you doing okay? You look tired."

She patted down her hair, which she hadn't had time to wash, and felt a little embarrassed. "My brother's wife had her baby last night. I didn't go to bed until three in the morning. So, yeah, I'm a little tired."

"Congratulations," he said with a smile. Tears formed in his eyes. "Mariela, right?"

She grinned. "Yep. And she's beautiful."

Markos sighed. "I'm sure that's true. And everything went okay with the delivery? There were no problems?"

"No problems," Denise said. "She's the most perfect baby I've ever seen."

"I'm sure she is. Wonderful. Congratulations again. Please give my best wishes to her parents—and to your father."

Denise froze. Why would Professor Nadir mention only her father? How did he know that her *mother* wasn't in the picture?

"What's wrong, Denise? You look faint," Markos said.

"I, um…" She backed away. "It's nothing."

She glanced around the lecture hall to find they were alone.

"I'm looking forward to coffee on Wednesday. And I'd love to see a photo of your niece."

"Okay. Sounds good." She hurried from the lecture hall, unsure now of how she felt about Markos Nadir.

CHAPTER FOUR

First Date

Markos was waiting for Denise at a table on the Starbucks patio when she arrived on Wednesday morning. He smiled up at her as he stood, and she was surprised when he greeted her with an embrace.

"Thanks for meeting with me," he said as he pulled away, noticing her surprise.

The embrace had felt natural up until that moment, as though he'd done it a hundred times. Maybe he was thinking of his wife. Or, maybe this *was* an actual date.

It was a beautiful morning in San Antonio in late October, when the weather hadn't yet turned cold, and the heat of the summer was far behind them. Denise wore a light jacket, and so did Markos, but they would have been fine without them, as the mid-sixties' temperature was pleasant, and the winds were calm.

"Shall we?" he asked, as he held open the door.

They ordered lattes and decided to return to the table on the outside patio.

"How are your sister-in-law and niece doing?" he asked.

"Great." Denise took a sip of her latte and then pulled her phone from her purse. "Check it out."

She showed him photos of Mariela, taken just after she was born.

"It's hard to believe," he said.

"What do you mean?" she looked at the phone, too, and was aware of how close she was to Markos. She could feel his breath on her cheek.

"The miracle of life."

"Oh. Yeah." She laughed, putting her phone away. "But it's not quite as mind-blowing as time-travel."

"I think it is." He glanced at her sideways.

He was utterly attractive and looking at her now in the most non-creepy way imaginable. There had to be an explanation for what he had said after class on Monday, about congratulating her father and not her mother. She decided to confront him.

"So, Markos?" Calling him by his first name still felt thrilling.

"Yes?"

"How did you know about my mother?" she asked.

"What do you mean?" He wrinkled his thick brows, and his emerald eyes softened.

"You told me to congratulate my brother, sister-in-law, and father about Mariela, but you didn't mention my mother. How did you know she was gone?"

His face paled, a reaction that made adrenaline surge through her body. Maybe she should be afraid of him, after all.

"It was in your student file," he said. "When I take an interest in students, I like to learn as much as I can about them. I'm sorry if that makes you uneasy."

"My student file?" she tried to think back as to how he could have concluded that she was motherless from her file.

"You're very brilliant. One of my brightest students. I wanted to find out where you attended school—to see if you'd gone to a private, college prep school. You can imagine my surprise when I'd learned you attended a public school in one of the poorest districts in the area."

Denise sipped at her latte to hide her embarrassment.

"On the application, it asks about parents, and you marked that your father was living but not your mother," he said. "How did she die? Do you mind if I ask?"

She hadn't talked about what had happened—not ever. She and her father and brother spoke of her mother, but they never referred to the accident that killed her.

"I'll talk about my mother if you'll talk about your wife," she challenged.

He sucked in his lips and took a deep breath though his nose. As he exhaled, he nodded.

"You go first," Denise insisted.

"She died of lung cancer," he said.

Denise averted her eyes. "I'm so sorry."

"By the time the doctor discovered it, it was too late to treat. She died within a year of the diagnosis."

"How horrible." Denise resisted the urge to take his hand.

She was surprised when he squeezed hers.

"As soon as she received the diagnosis, I was desperate to find a cure. I was a doctor then, practicing medicine. But I should have…" He pounded a fist against his thigh. "I should have spent her last months by her side."

"You did what you thought was right."

He squeezed her hand again. "Thank you, Denise. You're a kind soul. Easy to talk to. I'm sure you always have been."

She blinked, again disconcerted by the feeling that he somehow knew her. When he released her hand to take another drink, she hid hers on her lap.

"Now tell me about your mother," he said gently. "It's probably something you never talk about."

"That's true." She wiped her eyes. "I've never told anyone or talked about what happened. My father shut down, and I had to be there for him."

"What about your brother?" Markos asked.

"He took it hard, too, but he was never as close to my father as I was." Denise rubbed her temples. A migraine was coming on.

"Are you okay?"

She nodded, wishing she hadn't made the deal to talk about their lost loved ones. "My dad shut down because it was his fault."

"Oh, God. I didn't know that."

"How could you?" she studied his face.

"What happened?"

Her stomach became nauseated, like it had after her mid-term exam. She pushed the latte away and leaned her elbows on the table, needing some extra support.

"Denise, you don't have to talk about this. You don't look well." He laid a hand on her shoulder.

She took comfort in his touch and folded her arms on the table and rested her head on one cheek, facing Markos with her eyes closed.

"I was fourteen years old," she said. "Girard was sixteen. Mom and Dad had rented a sailboat through Fort Sam and had taken us to Canyon Lake for the Fourth of July."

Tears poured from her eyes, and she felt panicky as she gasped for a breath.

Markos caressed her arm. "Are you okay?"

"I don't know. I feel weak. It's hard to breathe."

He caressed her back and leaned close. She opened her eyes and was comforted by the concern on his face.

"You don't have to do this," he said softly. "It's okay."

"It's something I probably need to do, but I don't know if I can."

He took his napkin and dabbed her cheeks. "Please don't cry. I don't like to see you this way."

The intimate contact and the way he was looking at her made her desperately want to kiss him. "Thank you. I'm okay. Really."

"Good, because it's almost time for class to begin. Why don't I drive, and I'll bring you back for your car later?"

"I have a class after yours."

"Come by my office when you're ready, and I'll bring you back. I don't want you to drive in this state, okay?"

"Okay. Thank you."

Denise found it difficult to concentrate during Markos's lecture, even though he had told her during the drive to campus that the material he would cover was important. But today he spoke about alternate worlds and parallel universes—the stuff of science fiction. He didn't seriously believe in these radical theories, did he?

When class was over and she was leaving the back exit, Brian caught up to her.

"You don't look so hot, Denise. Are you feeling sick?" he asked as he followed her from the lecture hall.

"I'm just getting over a bug, but I'll be fine."

She turned away in the opposite direction, toward her composition class. There was no reason to encourage Brian by making small talk. He needed to move on.

After her composition class, she returned to Chapman Hall, determined to tell Markos about her mother's accident. A deal was a deal. He'd told her about his wife's death, and it was time for Denise to keep her word. Besides, she probably should have talked to someone about this a very long time ago, and Markos had been so patient and understanding at Starbucks.

When she arrived at his office, his door was ajar, and another student was sitting in the chair closest to his desk, talking about today's lecture. She recognized the boy—one of the more talkative in their class. He seemed very excited about the theories surrounding parallel universes. Denise waited outside for fifteen minutes, listening in, not wanting to interrupt. She was struck by how patient and articulate Markos was with the student. He was an amazing teacher and an incredible man. She felt fortunate that he'd taken such an interest in her.

The student left after fifteen minutes.

"Oh, sorry about that," the student said when he noticed her waiting by the door.

"That's fine. No problem."

"See you in class."

"See you," she said.

"Denise, come in," Markos called from his desk as he climbed to his feet.

She closed the door behind her, not wanting to be overheard.

"How are you feeling? Any better?" he asked.

"I want to tell you what happened," she said. "Do you have time?"

"Yes, of course. But don't feel obligated. You don't have to, you know."

"Yes, I do. I've never told anyone before, and I feel I should. Maybe it will help."

"Please sit down," he said, motioning to the chair nearest his desk where the previous student had just been sitting moments before.

She took the seat, fighting tears. She was trembling and weak and trying hard to breathe.

"Take your time," he said. "Do you want some water?"

"No, it's okay. Thank you." She took a deep breath and released it slowly.

He leaned back in his chair and crossed an ankle over the other knee, waiting patiently for her to speak.

"Like I said this morning, it was the Fourth of July, about six years ago," she said. "My father used to sail with *his* father, but he hadn't had the opportunity in many years, and he thought it would be fun to take the family on the lake. He and my mom didn't make a lot of money, but we did okay, and since he was in the military, he could rent a sailboat at a good price. So, we did."

She took another deep breath and slowly released it as she squeezed her hands together.

"My father had been drinking. He used to get drunk all the time. I didn't think anything of it back then. It was a holiday, and lots of people were drinking on the lake."

"That's not unusual," Markos said.

"But no one else on the boat knew how to control it." Denise bit her lip, fighting the tears and the tightness in her throat. "Only he knew what to do. And when he got too drunk to handle the boat, he got mad at Girard and told him he needed to be a man and sail the boat."

"Oh," Markos muttered.

"My dad could barely stand, and the wind had picked up. He was yelling at us to take down the sail, but we didn't know how. My mom tried to keep us calm and didn't see the jet ski. We were heading straight for it. Dad hollered out to the kid driving it, but the kid thought we were waving and didn't know we had lost control. Just as we hit, the boy jumped from his jet ski, but my mother…"

"Oh, no." Markos stood up and put a hand on her shoulder.

"I can still see her, flying from the boat and crashing into the jet ski." Her throat tightened. She could barely speak.

"Oh, God."

Denise looked up at him, allowing the tears to escape. "At first, my dad blamed my brother. And Girard was miserable. I think he blamed himself, too. He and my dad had the most terrible fights back then."

"I'm so sorry. I didn't know."

"My dad's drinking got so bad that we had to have him admitted. He was gone for six months. It was just me and Girard. My Aunt Latisha checked in on us each day, but I was so lonely and so sad. My whole world had fallen apart."

"Oh, Denise."

"It's amazing that Girard and I turned out as well as we did. He's an investment broker with a large firm and married to a successful attorney. And I got into one of the best schools in the country. I guess we both poured ourselves into our studies to escape the lack of a home life."

Markos went down on one knee and stroked her hair, then her cheek. She closed her eyes, grateful for the comfort, for the affection, and unsure what it all meant. Shivers of delight swept through her body, overcoming the feelings of sadness and loss.

"My father was given some medicine for depression, but he never fully recovered," she said. "He stays in his room all day and night and rarely comes out. I've had to take care of him ever since."

"You poor thing," he caressed her back. "I knew you were a strong woman. In fact, you inspired me…" His voice dropped off.

"What? How?" His words made no sense to her whatsoever.

"Brilliant students like you inspire me to be a better person, a better teacher. You are the future, Denise. And your past, as difficult as it was, shaped you into the strong woman you've become."

"Oh." She wanted to kiss him. She honest-to-God had never wanted anything more. But when she gazed longingly at his mouth, he stood up and returned to the chair behind his desk.

Then he crossed one ankle over a knee and leaned back again, steepling his fingers. "There are new drugs for depression that can help your father."

"Wouldn't his doctor prescribe what was best for him?" she asked.

"New medicines not on the market yet, not available to the general population. But I have contacts that would allow me to get ahold of some."

"I don't want him to take anything experimental. I mean, he's housebound, but he's doing okay."

"He could be better. These drugs are aimed at PTSD, which is the main cause of your father's condition."

"You sound like a medical doctor."

"I did practice medicine, remember? I told you that, didn't I? I practiced medicine until I was twenty-six."

"And how old are you now?" she asked.

"Twenty-eight."

She studied the sharp lines of his face, his kind and sincere eyes. "I'll talk to my dad about it tonight and let you know."

"Excellent. Are you ready to get your car then?"

She climbed to her feet, unsteadily, but she held the desk until the dizziness stopped. "Yes, thanks."

Markos put an arm around her waist as they walked to the elevator. His touch made her feel dizzier.

"Aren't you worried what people will think?" she whispered.

"No. That's the last thing on my mind." He winked down at her.

She was unsure how to take that comment, but, nevertheless, she was exhilarated and charmed to the bone. She was falling for this man—hard. She hoped she wouldn't get hurt.

As he drove her to her car, he told her to call him when her father was ready, and he would get the right medicine and deliver it to her house.

"I don't usually make house calls, but I think I can make an exception this once," he said.

"I'll cook for you," she said. "We'll have you over for our Sunday dinner, and you can meet my brother and his family, too."

He gave her a genuine smile. "I'd like that very much."

That evening, Denise made tacos using the pork roast she had been cooking in the crockpot all day. She had picked up fresh flour tortillas from a local restaurant on the way home from school and now garnished the tacos with shredded cheddar, sour cream, and slices of avocado. She filled plates for her and her father and carried them to his room, like she did nearly every night.

"What smells so delicious?" he asked as she walked in.

"Haven't you been smelling it all day?" she asked, handing him his plate.

"Indeed, I have. I was wondering what smelled so good. Hmm—hmm, Baby. Thank you."

"You're welcome, Daddy." She sat in her chair and glanced at the television. "The History Channel again?"

"Is there something else you want to watch? You can change it, if you want."

"No, Daddy, that's okay. I want to talk, if that's alright."

"Sure, Baby. What's on your mind?"

"You remember that professor you wanted me to invite over for dinner?"

"I knew it!" he said pointing a finger at her. "I told you so. Didn't I?"

Denise laughed. "You sure did. I thought you were crazy, but you were right."

"Well, we *know* I'm crazy. But I can still call it like it is."

"Oh, Daddy."

"So, when's he coming?"

"This Sunday. I'm going to invite the whole family, okay? I'll make filled noodles again, if that's alright."

"You'll get no complaints from me. You know that's my favorite."

Denise decided not to tell her father everything she had told Markos that day, but she did tell him about the medicine. "He's a cutting-edge scientist and a doctor, Daddy. I think we should trust him."

"I'm sure he is, but are there side effects or other things we should be worried about? I feel fine already."

"Daddy, you aren't fine. If there's a way to help you, we should try it."

Her father frowned. "I know taking care of me hasn't been easy for you."

"I'm glad to do it. Please don't cry."

He covered his eyes with one hand. "I'm a grown man and my baby girl has to do everything for me."

"You can't help that you're sick. Please, Daddy. It's okay. And Markos, he can help you."

Her father nodded but kept his hand over his eyes. He refused to look at her.

She finished eating in silence, and, when she was full, she got up. "You want me to take your plate, or are you still eating?"

"Take it, Baby. I'll eat more tomorrow."

She leaned over and kissed the top of his head. "I love you, Daddy. I like taking care of you. I just worry, that's all. I want you to have a better life."

He wiped his eyes and finally looked at her. "Oh, I know it. I do. Thank you. I'll try the medicine, okay? I'll do it for you."

She kissed his cheek. "Thank you, Daddy. Good night."

"Good night."

CHAPTER FIVE

Second Date

Markos was the first guest to arrive on Sunday, a few minutes before noon. He embraced Denise at the door, just as he had on the patio of Starbucks, and it felt even more natural this time, since Denise wasn't taken by surprise. But she *was* surprised when Markos also hugged her father and told him how happy he was to finally meet him.

Her father sat with Markos in the living room while Denise finished up in the kitchen. She was just heating up the rolls and spreading icing on the cake. The tea and coffee were made, and the pot of filled noodles was simmering.

She was happy—happier than she'd been in a long, long time.

When the doorbell rang again, Denise rushed to greet her brother, his wife, and baby Mariela, excited to introduce them to Markos.

Markos seemed excited, too—even nervous.

He shook Girard's hand and said, "You look so young."

"Thank you, I think?" Girard laughed.

Denise had always thought her brother was very attractive, with their father's pleasant eyes and stout build and their mother's fine hair. With fine black hair and lighter skin, he looked more Hispanic, like Kassia, than white or black, but he looked enough like Denise that people could tell they were siblings.

Markos embraced Kassia, almost as if he already knew her. "You're so beautiful." Then he quickly added, "She has the glow of a new mother."

"Thank you," Kassia said, before kissing the soft black hair on her baby's head. "And this is our Mariela."

Markos's eyes became wet with tears.

"She's precious," he said. "And unbelievably tiny."

He touched her little hand, and baby Mariela grabbed his finger.

To everyone's surprise, Markos broke into tears.

"Markos?" Denise put a hand on his lower back. "Are you okay?"

"Yes, yes. I'm sorry I'm so emotional."

Denise wondered if her niece reminded him of what he could have had with his late wife.

"That's okay, man," Girard said. "You should have seen me! I bawled like a baby when I first met her!"

"Me, too," Denise's father said. "Babies do that to folks."

"They're certainly little miracles, aren't they?" Markos said, gazing once more at Mariela. Then, to Kassia, he said, "Congratulations, Mrs. Walker."

"Kassia," Kassia said. "Would you like to hold her?"

Markos wiped his eyes and nodded. Kassia gingerly passed her little bundle over to Markos, and he cupped the baby in his arms and gazed down at her. He was trembling like a new father. After a few moments of looking with utter fascination at little Mariela, he buried his head in her blanket and sobbed.

Denise glanced around at her family members, not sure what to do or say.

"I have a feeling Mariela is going to have that effect on a lot of young men," Denise's father said.

Girard laughed. "But hopefully not for a very long time."

Markos wiped his tears on his jacket at each shoulder. "My apologies. I suppose I can't wait to be a father myself one day."

Kassia secretly winked at Denise behind Markos's back, as if to say, "He's ready."

"Why don't we sit at the table?" Denise suggested, to hide her embarrassment over Kassia's wink, which had been witnessed by Girard and their father. "Everything's ready."

"What about Aunt Latisha?" Girard asked. "Isn't she coming?"

"She wasn't feeling up to it," Denise said. "Her back's bothering her again."

"That's too bad," Markos said. "I was looking forward to meeting her."

"I'm going to lay the baby down in the spare room." Kassia took Mariela from Markos's arms. "I'll be right back."

Once everyone had been served and a blessing said by her father, Markos said, "Mmm. Filled noodles. One of my favorites. This is a real treat."

"You've had them before?" Denise's father asked.

"Many times," Markos replied. "But none as tasty as these."

Denise blushed. "Thanks. I'm glad you like them. My mother used to make them all the time."

"This is a German recipe that has been in my wife's family for many generations," her father explained.

"I might need a second bowl," Markos said with a smile.

"Be sure to save room for cake," her father warned.

"You baked a cake?" Girard asked. "She must really like you, Markos."

Denise laughed nervously. "Don't act like I never bake."

"Between work and school and taking care of me, it's a wonder she bakes at all," her father said. "She's a good cook, too. I should know." Her father patted his small, pot belly and everyone laughed.

"What kind of cake did you make, Denise?" Kassia asked.

"Lemon cream," she said after swallowing her bite.

"You made your famous lemon cream cake?" Markos said with astonishment.

"I wouldn't call it *famous*," she said, blushing again. "It's the first time I've made it. Are you teasing me?"

"Just feeling optimistic," he said with a wink. "I have a feeling it will be famous in this family one day."

"I'll be the judge of that," her father said. "As soon as I'm done with this masterpiece." He indicated his bowl of filled noodles.

"Mmm-mm," Girard said.

It was quiet for a minute or two, as everyone ate.

Denise's father broke the silence and said, "I want to hear about these ideas of yours, Markos. Denise has told me a little. Objects moving faster than the speed of light…"

"That's not possible," Girard said. "Is it?"

"It most definitely is," Markos replied. "You can measure their movement by the…"

"Shimmering effect they leave behind," Denise finished for him.

"Very good, Denise," Markos said.

"Gravitational waving," Denise explained. "The traveling object affects the things around it in its wake."

"How interesting," her father said. "And Denise also spoke recently about time travel, something about wormholes."

"Traversing wormholes, yes," Markos said. "But even more important than the unpredictable wormholes are…"

"Closed time-like curves," Denise finished for him again.

"You really *have* been paying attention," Markos said.

Denise explained the concept to the others.

"I knew it!" Girard said. "I knew I would time travel one day. I just had a feeling."

"Oh, stop," Kassia laughed. "You and your comic books."

"You never know," Markos said with a smile.

"Don't make fun of my comics," Girard said to Kassia. "Little Mariela is gonna be a comic fan, too, someday. You just wait and see."

"I have a feeling you're right," Markos said before he took another bite.

Once everyone had finished, Girard offered to clear the dinner bowls away to make room for the cake plates, which Kassia set out as Denise carried the cake to the table. Just then, Mariela started fussing in the other room, so Kassia excused herself.

"Yum," Denise's father said after taking a bite of the lemon cream cake. "I do believe this cake will be famous, Markos. You called it right, my man."

"It's the best cake I've ever tasted," Markos said. "I'm very grateful that you all welcomed me into your home. This is the best meal, and best company, I've had in years. I *mean* that."

Denise's father raised his eyebrows at her and gave her a cheesy grin. Girard even eye-balled her with innuendo.

She laughed with joy and said, "Thank you, Markos. What a nice thing to say."

Kassia then returned to the table with Mariela in her arms.

"Can I hold her while you finish your cake?" Denise offered.

"Sure." Kassia came around the table and handed the baby over.

Denise cuddled the sweet thing. "She really is precious."

Markos took Mariela's little hand and kissed it. "She really is."

Then he shocked her by leaning over and kissing Denise on the cheek, in front of God and everyone.

"She takes after her aunt," he said.

After Girard and Kassia had left with Mariela, Denise sat in the living room on the sofa beside Markos. Her father sat across from them on the loveseat.

"This medicine will make you feel a million times better," Markos was explaining. "But it will take at least two weeks before you feel a significant impact."

"Alright," her father said.

Denise could tell her father was skeptical and a little afraid and was pushing himself to do it for her.

"Daily exercise will dramatically increase the effectiveness of the medication," Markos added. "Even if it's just a twenty-minute stroll around the block."

Her father lifted his brows. He hadn't left the house in years, not even to go outside to get the mail, except to go for his annual checkup with their family doctor.

"Hmmm. We'll see about that," her father said.

Markos handed over the bottle of pills. "Take one each morning—not at night, okay? They're recommended for morning because they contain caffeine and might keep you awake at night."

"He doesn't need any help with that," Denise said. "He doesn't sleep much."

"You didn't mention that," Markos said. "I can give him something that will help with that, too."

"Let's just start with this and see how it goes," her father said.

"Fair enough," Markos said. "If you don't mind, I'll check on you in about three weeks? And if you have any problems before then, you can give me a call, or contact me through Denise."

Markos handed her father a card. "This has my personal cell phone number on it. Feel free to call me anytime, for any reason."

"Well, thank you, Markos," her father said. "That's awfully kind of you. But you better not break my daughter's heart."

"Daddy!" Denise felt the blood rush to her cheeks as she noticed Markos's face pale.

"I wouldn't dream of it," Markos finally said.

Later, when she walked him to his car in the early evening, he put his hands on her shoulders and said, "Thank you for a lovely afternoon. I was serious about what I said. The best meal. The best company. I'd love to take you out to dinner sometime, to repay you for your kindness."

"There's no need to repay me. You just helped my father."

"Then I'd love to take you out anyway. Would that be okay with you?"

She beamed up at him. "Sure."

"How about next Friday night? Don't you love steak?"

"Yes, I do." She wondered how he knew that. Had she mentioned it to him? It was the one thing she didn't know how to cook and wished she could have more often.

"I found a really good steakhouse on the other side of town. Why don't I pick you up here on Friday around seven?"

"Sounds great. I look forward to it."

As he was still holding her by the shoulders, she thought he would kiss her and was disappointed when he didn't.

"Fantastic," he said, pulling away to open his car door. "I'll see you in class tomorrow."

"See you then."

Later, after she'd finished her calculus homework and edited a paper for Composition, she ate leftovers with her father in his room with the History Channel playing.

They'd been quietly eating, when her father broke the silence and said, "Markos is a fine young man. He seems to fit in well with our family."

"I'm glad you approve, Daddy." She flashed him an involuntary smile. "I don't think I've ever liked someone quite as much as I do him."

"Just be careful. He *is* older than you and more experienced."

"I know. You were older than Mom."

"True. How old is Markos, do you know?"

"Twenty-eight."

"A lot of things can happen in a young person's life between the ages of twenty and twenty-eight. I like Markos. I do. Just proceed with caution. That's all I'm saying, Baby."

"I will, Daddy."

Denise didn't fall asleep right away that night, because she kept reliving the dinner with Markos over and over in her mind. She loved how sweet he was with her family, especially with Mariela, and how kind he was to her father. She was most excited by the way he had kissed her on the cheek in front of her entire family. If that wasn't a sign that he was interested in taking their relationship to the next level, she didn't know what was.

But her father was right: she was twenty, and Markos was twenty-eight, and Denise needed to proceed with caution.

CHAPTER SIX

Third Date

Denise was nervous on the way to the steakhouse in the car with Markos, because in class all week, he'd seemed different—less warm, more distant. She supposed he had to be that way in front of the other students, but, up until then, he hadn't seemed to care about what others thought. And tonight, when he had picked her up from her house, he hadn't embraced her, like he had at Starbucks and at her Sunday family dinner.

He looked handsome in his green turtleneck and blue jeans, and it was with great self-control that she didn't keep stealing glances at him as he drove. He was quiet, even somber, adding to her feelings of anxiety.

The first cold front of autumn had finally blown in, and she wrapped her coat closely around her—not because she was cold in the toasty car, but because she was afraid.

"Are you cold?" he asked, noticing her shiver.

"No. I'm fine. Thanks."

"What about this music?" he asked. "Is it okay?"

"It's fine. Nice, even."

She rarely listened to contemporary jazz, but she liked it.

"I never get tired of these oldies," he said.

"Oh, I thought this was contemporary. Shows you what I know about jazz."

"No, you're right," he said. "This particular band *is* contemporary. Music is probably this generation's greatest contribution to humankind."

That seemed like an odd thing to say, but she giggled and said, "You're probably right."

When it became silent between them again, she said, "So, other than jazz, what other interests or hobbies do you have?"

"Scuba diving."

This was a surprise. "I've always wanted to learn."

"I have a yacht off the coast of Guam, and I go to it every chance I get."

"Sounds incredible."

"It is."

"I've always loved the ocean and ocean life. Scuba diving is on my bucket list. You're lucky."

"Maybe you'd like to go with me over Spring Break. I could teach you."

Denise's confidence level soared. He must like her a lot to make such an offer—unless he was just blowing smoke. "I would like that very much."

She found herself smiling all through dinner as they ate and laughed together, talking about everything under the sun. In addition to jazz music and scuba diving, Markos also enjoyed fishing, golfing, and hiking—though, according to Markos, the golf courses where he was from were much better than those in San Antonio.

"And where is that?" she asked. "New York City?"

"My family is originally from Egypt, and, although I was born in New York, I've lived all over."

"Oh?" she took a sip of her iced tea. "And, so far, what's been your favorite place to live?"

"San Antonio," he replied.

"Even though the golf courses aren't as good, and it's so far away from your yacht?"

He smiled solemnly. "Yes. You see, this is where my wife was born, and we lived here together before…before I left…before I taught at Harvard."

He avoided her eyes as he moved the food around on his plate.

"I'm sorry," she said, looking at her plate, too.

The drive back to her house was quiet again, but Denise's confidence hadn't waivered. She realized that she must be the first woman he had dated since his wife's death and that all of this was difficult for him. She would be patient. Markos Nadir was worth however long it would take for his heart to open up to hers.

When they reached her house, she said, "If you have any room for dessert, there's still some of that lemon cream cake from Sunday."

"I always have room for your famous lemon cream cake."

She laughed. It was so funny for him to call it *famous* when it was the first time she'd ever made it.

While she sliced him a piece from the refrigerator, he went to her father's room to check on him.

Markos returned a few moments later and said, "I can already see the medication is helping."

"Oh? In what way?" she asked.

"He's showered and shaved. Looks like a new man, if you ask me."

Denise's jaw dropped open. She usually had to coax her father into a bath. He'd stopped grooming himself years ago. She'd had to force him to let her cut his hair every few months. He never cared how badly he smelled, even though she'd told him he should bathe for her sake, if not for his own.

She left the kitchen table, where she'd served Markos his cake and rushed to her father's room. He was out of bed, in her chair, reading a book! He hadn't read a book in years. His face looked as smooth as a baby's bottom. He looked handsome and ten years younger.

"Daddy?"

He smiled up at her. "Well. Hello, Baby. I just spoke to Markos. Did you have a nice time?"

"I sure did. He's having a piece of lemon cream cake right now. You want a piece?"

"Sure." He got up from her chair.

"I'll bring it to you," she offered.

"That's okay. I'll join you, if that's alright."

Denise inwardly laughed at the irony. The one time she wanted her dad to stay in his room, he insisted on coming out. But she was glad that he seemed to be feeling better already.

"Of course," she said. "Come on."

She brewed a pot of coffee, and the three of them visited for an hour before her father finally excused himself and returned to his room. Denise asked Markos if he'd like to watch a little television, but he said no, he should probably go. She walked him to his car, hoping he'd give her a kiss. She was screwing up the courage to initiate the kiss, when they stopped at his car door.

"Markos?" she said, moving closer to him in the chilly night.

"Yes?" He stuffed his hands in his coat pockets.

"Thank you for tonight. I had a great time."

"I did, too. Thanks for the cake and for the great company."

"I'm glad you enjoyed it."

He moved closer, putting a hand on her shoulder.

"I can't tell you how lonely I've been, Denise. For years, since Mariela's death, I was so lonely."

She moved her hand to cover his on her shoulder. "I'm sorry you've been feeling that way. If it's any consolation, I'm growing very fond of you."

"The feeling's mutual, I assure you," he said softly.

With her heart racing, she lifted her chin, gazing at his luscious lips.

But when he embraced her, it was not to touch his lips to hers. He held her head to his chest and said gently, "I want to kiss you so badly.

God knows how badly I want to. I've been so alone, so miserable. But I can't. I just can't."

The only thing she could think to say was, "I'm sorry." She whispered it against the soft lapel of his jacket.

He moved his finger beneath her chin and lifted her face to his. He gazed down at her, his emerald eyes sparkling in the starlight. "You have nothing to be sorry for, sweet Denise. I knew you were an incredible woman, and I always wondered why you never married, but I understand now. You're devoted to your father, and without the proper medicine, he needed you."

She furrowed her brows. "Never married? Markos, I'm only twenty years old."

He sighed and shook his head. "I know. It's just that most women with your looks, your brains, and your disposition have boyfriends or fiancés by now."

She smiled. "That's sweet of you to say."

"What can I say? I'm a sweet man."

She laughed. "I realize this must be hard for you."

"You have no idea how hard." His voice was full of agony.

Looking up at him, she asked, "What about your family? Have they not been supportive since…?"

He shook his head. "Our relationship is very different now. It's hard to explain."

"Where do your parents live?" she asked.

"They're still in New York City," he said. "Maybe I'll show them to you someday."

She frowned, wondering why he had worded it that way—*show* instead of *introduce*. "Do you not speak to them anymore?"

"Like I said, our relationship is different now."

Her heart was moved by the greatest pity for him. "Oh, Markos."

"So, you see? You and your family have been like a lifeline for me— like a shot of medicine straight to the heart."

She wrapped her arms around his neck and pressed her body against his as she was overcome with both sadness and joy.

"You're shivering." He tightened his arms around her, and it felt magnificent to be held by him. "Let me walk you to the door."

She wanted to beg him to stay, to say she didn't mind the cold. She wasn't ready for him to leave, but when he turned her toward her sidewalk, she yielded.

He hugged her tightly once more on the front porch. She felt the desire in his breath, in his heartbeat, and in the deepness of his voice when he said, "Goodnight, Denise."

"Goodnight, Markos."

She watched him turn away toward his car, parked on the curb. She waited for him to start the engine and turn on the headlights before she waved once more and went inside.

Still no kiss—at least not on the lips—but certainly progress.

Denise went directly to her father's room, hoping for a chat before bed, but she discovered him asleep. He'd never been able to fall asleep before one or two in the morning—not since her mother had passed away six years ago. He'd changed into clean pajamas and had crawled into bed and was snoring as if he'd already fallen into the deepest slumber.

Her heart felt like it would burst with joy. Markos's medicine was going to give her father a new life, and, in so doing, it was going to do the same for her.

The next two weeks went by quickly as Denise worked on assignments that were due before Thanksgiving. She was also busy at work, because everyone wanted to look their best for the holidays. Despite how busy she was, Denise was disappointed that Markos hadn't asked her for another date. It confused her, especially when he had talked about taking her on his yacht for Spring Break and showing her his family someday in

New York City. Why would a man unsure of his feelings say such things that he must know would build expectations and give a woman hope?

She reminded herself that she needed to be patient. He'd been alone since his wife's death, and who knew what his dating life had been like before then? He wasn't used to relationships. Maybe she needed to take theirs by the reins.

So, on the Friday before Thanksgiving Break, she went by his office after her composition class and found him alone, with his door ajar, reading from a handheld device—not a phone or an iPad, but a cube-shaped device she'd never seen before. He wore a look of anxiety, something she wasn't used to seeing on his features.

She tapped the door, and he quickly put the device in the top drawer of his desk. "Come in. Come in. How nice of you to drop by."

His tone lacked intimacy altogether. He might have been talking to any other student.

"Is everything okay?" she asked. "You looked upset just now."

He frowned. "Not upset, frustrated. Well, maybe *upset* is the right word."

She moved closer to his desk. "Has something happened?"

"I'm a doctor and a scientist, and…"

She watched him struggle for the right words.

"There's so much more good I could be doing, but it would be at the cost of my own happiness. And yet choosing my own happiness over self-sacrifice sometimes makes me feel…"

"Guilty?"

"Yes. Guilty."

"Oh, Markos." She reached over and touched his hand. "You don't have to carry the weight of the world on your shoulders. Let the rest of us help."

He stood up, came around the desk, and took her hand, holding it close to his heart. "Have you always been so wise?"

She laughed nervously, pleased to be close to him again. "I doubt it."

When he still didn't ask her for a date this weekend, she swallowed hard and said, "My father and I would like you to join us for Thanksgiving, if you don't have other plans. My brother and his family and Aunt Latisha will be there."

She was surprised to see tears fill his eyes as he muttered, "I never got to meet Aunt Latisha."

"No, her back was hurting her that day you came for dinner, but she's feeling better."

He cleared his throat and rubbed his eyes, letting go of her hand.

"Sorry, I think I'm allergic to something in the air." He took a tissue from a box on the file cabinet and wiped his eyes and nose before stuffing the tissue into his trouser pocket. "I would love to join you and your family. Nothing sounds better to me at this moment."

"Oh, good!" She clapped her hands. "Plan to come at noon for turkey and dressing, but we eat again around five, so it's kind of an all-day affair."

"Will there be more of your famous lemon cream cake?" he asked with a grin.

"There *can* be. I usually make pies, but I can make the cake, too."

"You don't have to go to the trouble."

"Are you kidding?" she pecked his cheek. "I love doing things for you."

His teasing grin turned into a serious gaze as he glanced over the features of her face. Her body responded as she watched him looking at her with what she sincerely hoped was desire—the same desire she felt for him.

He looked about to kiss her.

Unaware that she was doing it, she pressed her body against his and reached her face up to his, and then remembering what he had said about not being able to kiss her, she reached her lips to his ear and whispered, "I'm a patient person. I'll wait for you, for however long it takes."

His arms were suddenly around her waist and holding her ever so tight. "Oh, sweet Denise."

He held her for many wonderful minutes before he finally pulled away and smiled down at her. "I have to go out of town for a few days on some business. I wish I could take you with me—one day I hope to take you there. It's an amazing place but difficult to get to."

So that was why he hadn't asked her out. "Where are you going?"

"It's hard to explain, but, like I said, I hope to show you someday."

"Out of state? Out of the country?"

"Yes. But before you leave, I just want to make sure you understood this week's focus on the planet's magnetism and the global magnetic reversals I went over in class."

"You mean how the north and south poles switch magnetism? Yes, I understood. Do you really think another reversal will happen in our life-time?"

"I'm sure it will," he said. "And I'm working hard to help other scientists better predict the exact time, so we can be better prepared."

"How can you predict such a thing? And how prepared do we need to be? Are you talking about cataclysmic destruction?"

He put his hands on her shoulders. "No, Nothing like that. It will, however, have a devastating impact on our technology if we don't prepare for the enormous electromagnetic wave that will hit. And we can use our understanding of what's happening in the earth's core to make our predictions."

"Is this why you're going out of town, to work on this problem?"

"Yes. But I promise to be back in time for Thanksgiving. Deal?"

She smiled up at him. "Deal."

"Oh, before you go, there's something I want to give you." He moved his hands behind his neck and unclasped a necklace that had been tucked beneath his shirt. "May I?"

She turned around so he could put on her. "What is it?"

"This necklace belonged to my wife, Mariela," he said. "It was a family heirloom passed down to her."

She turned to face him, shocked that he would give her something so personal from his wife. "But, Markos, shouldn't you keep this for yourself?"

"I have other keepsakes to remember her by. This is a *woman*'s necklace, and I feel you should have it."

She lifted the pendant that hung between her breasts. It was a teardrop blue sapphire with a border of white diamonds. It was exactly like a necklace belonging to her Aunt Latisha, though her aunt's pendant was on a different chain. Denise had often admired it. "It's so beautiful. I can't believe you're giving this to *me*. It must be worth…"

"It's finally where it belongs," he said. "And it looks lovely on you, Denise."

He must really care for her to give her such a valuable and sentimental gift. She felt exhilarated but speechless, and, if he didn't hurry up and kiss her, she was going to scream. She smiled up at him. But no kiss came.

She stifled the scream, clutched the pendant, and thanked him. "How very generous of you. I promise to take good care of it."

"I look forward to seeing you as soon as I get back."

That was her cue to leave. "Have a safe trip, Markos."

He squeezed her shoulders. "Thanks. I'll see you soon."

CHAPTER SEVEN

First Kiss

Denise was worried on Thanksgiving Day, after Girard and his family and Aunt Latisha had already arrived and had been waiting over an hour to be served, when there was no sign of Markos. He hadn't returned her call or text.

Her first thought was that his return trip had been delayed. Maybe he ran into bad weather.

Her second thought was that maybe he couldn't celebrate a holiday he once enjoyed with his wife.

Her third thought was, screw it, we're eating, and she told everyone to come to the table and sit down.

"Let's give your young man a few more minutes," Aunt Latisha objected.

Denise's aunt was a thin, pear-shaped woman with wide hips and saggy arms and a youthful smile. Although she would be turning sixty in January, she gave the impression of being ten years younger—except when her back was hurting. Today, she looked energized, her brown eyes as sparkly as the pendant she wore around her neck.

It hadn't gone unnoticed that Denise was wearing a pendant that looked exactly like Aunt Latisha's, but everyone in the family had agreed that it was one more sign that Denise and Markos were a match made in heaven.

"I don't want Kassia's mashed potatoes or your green bean casserole to get cold," Denise told her aunt. "I'm sure he'll understand."

Everyone made their way to the table as Denise put the turkey and sides on the crocheted runner down the center. Mariela was still asleep in her carrier, as she had been when Kassia and Girard had arrived.

"I hope he comes," Aunt Latisha said. "I was looking forward to meeting him."

"I'm sure he'll come," Denise's father said. "Or he'll have a good reason."

"He better," Girard said. "No one disappoints my baby sister without hearing something about it."

"Oh, Girard," Kassia said.

"Can we change the subject?" Denise asked. "Why don't we go around the table and say what we're most thankful for this year?"

It was no surprise that everyone in the family was thankful for the same thing: Mariela; however, Aunt Latisha added, "And for the healing of my little brother. I will be forever grateful to your young man, Denise. I've not seen Duane this lively and handsome in years."

"Thank you, Sis," Denise's father said. "I'm thankful for that, too. I may even be well enough to go back to work."

Denise's mouth fell open. "Are you serious, Daddy?"

"Yes, I am. I have a friend who's retired military, and he went through a program to become a schoolteacher. I think I'd like to look into that."

"You'd make a great teacher, Duane," Aunt Latisha said.

Everyone else agreed, too.

They were about halfway through their meal, when the front door suddenly burst open, and Markos ran to the table, crying, "Am I too late?"

Denise stood up and laughed nervously at his strange behavior as she closed the door behind him. "There's plenty of food, Markos. Why don't you come and sit down?"

Markos was carrying a black case, and, instead of sitting, he went to one end of the table, where Aunt Latisha sat.

"You must be Aunt Latisha," he said, smiling down at her.

"Hello, Markos," she said, giving him her hand. "It's nice to finally meet you."

"Oh, dear," he said, looking first at her arm and then at her face. "Listen to me. You know I'm a medical doctor, right?"

"Why, yes," Latisha said.

"She sees the proof right there." Girard pointed at their father.

"Then you'll trust me when I tell you that you need to start taking medication right away." Markos set his black case on the table beside his empty plate and took out a bottle of pills."

"But I feel just fine," Aunt Latisha insisted.

"Markos?" Denise asked. "What's this about? What do you think is wrong with my aunt?"

"If she doesn't take this first dose immediately, she'll have a heart attack today. I'm certain of it."

Denise's father, who sat on the opposite end of the table from Aunt Latisha, stood up. "How can you tell that just by looking at her?"

Markos sucked in his lips and sighed as he turned to her father. "I helped you, didn't I? You're feeling better now, aren't you?"

"Yes, but…"

"Trust me on this, please? She needs to take one of these now." Markos opened the pill bottle and handed a capsule to Aunt Latisha. "Please?"

"What's in it?" Aunt Latisha studied the capsule. "Are there any side effects?"

"The only side effect is that it will save your life," Markos said anxiously. "You do want to live, don't you?"

"Markos!" Denise went to his side. "Why are you acting this way?"

"Because when I look at your aunt, I see death—imminent death. Please take the pill, Latisha."

Denise nodded at her aunt. "Please. He must know what he's talking about."

Latisha popped the capsule into her mouth before swallowing a gulp of iced tea.

Markos sighed with relief. "Thank God. I had to go to the moon and back to get those. I wasn't sure I'd make it in time."

"What are you talking about?" Girard asked.

"Figuratively speaking, of course," Markos added.

"But how did you know she'd need them?" Kassia asked.

"That's what I want to know," Denise's father added.

"I didn't." Markos sat down in the empty chair next to where Denise had been sitting, and he squeezed her hand as she took her seat beside him. "I didn't know. Of course, not. But I needed to get them for someone else, and I got held up. I was worried I wouldn't get here before everyone left."

"Well, you made it," Latisha said, patting his free hand. "And thank you for being so concerned about me. I'm sure I'm fine, but if you say I need to take these pills, I'll take them."

"One each night before bedtime," Markos said.

"Now let's get you some turkey and dressing," Denise said.

Later, after their second meal and another round of dessert, including lemon cream cake, after the football game had ended, and Baby Mariela had grown too fussy to console, everyone said their goodbyes except for Markos. Denise's father sat with them for another half hour, sipping coffee, before he said goodnight and retreated to his room.

Alone with Markos on the living room sofa, Denise turned to him and asked, "So tell me more about your trip."

"Oh, there's nothing to tell."

"Seriously? What about the problem of the planet's reverse magnetism? Were you able to come up with a plan?"

"Yes, as a matter of fact." He smiled down at her. "I'm happy to report that I was able to bring back an electromagnetic stabilizer that will prevent our electronic devices from exploding."

"That's good news," she said with a chuckle. "Otherwise, it would have been terribly inconvenient."

He laughed with her and then suddenly cupped her cheek, sending chills throughout her body. "You don't realize it, but you're the reason I was able to accomplish it."

She jerked her chin back in surprise. "Me? How?"

"You're my muse, Denise. My inspiration. It's taken me a while to fully understand that."

She gazed at his mouth with longing, trying to be patient, and then she laughed and said, "I think I need a personal electromagnetic stabilizer, Markos."

He laughed, too. "What do you mean?"

"I feel like I'm about to explode." And with that, she pressed her lips to his.

He returned her kiss, cupping her face with both hands, and she wrapped her arms around his waist and pulled him closer. Feverishly, she kissed him like she had never kissed a single soul before.

"Oh, Denise," he whispered.

"Don't stop." She pressed her mouth to his once more and relished the feel of his silky lips and smooth tongue. "Don't ever stop."

When Markos left an hour later, Denise sat alone in the living room remembering all that had happened that day: Markos arriving late to their Thanksgiving dinner, bursting through the door and insisting that Aunt Latisha take a new medicine to avoid a heart attack; the wonderful visit they had together with her family, especially the way he had held Baby Mariela and cooed at her as if he couldn't wait to be a father…

And then there were those kisses of ecstasy that had Denise longing for more of him. She'd wished the night would never end, but here it was: over. Had it really happened? Or had she dreamed it? She clutched the sapphire pendant that hung between her breasts.

"This is happening," she whispered with a smile.

Denise didn't hear from Markos for the remainder of the Thanksgiving Break. She thought about calling him a hundred times, but didn't want to come across as needy, impatient, or pushy. So, when it came time for class on Monday morning, she felt shy and nervous about seeing him.

As always, as soon as he'd entered the lecture hall at the start of class, he sought her among the students in the audience. His smile, however, lacked the usual joy and excitement today. It even appeared grim. Denise couldn't imagine what could have possibly changed between their luscious encounter last Thursday night and today. Why did this man continually give her such mixed signals?

She clutched the sapphire pendant and reminded herself that no man would give a woman such an expensive piece of jewelry that had once belonged to his deceased wife if he didn't have strong feelings for her.

When class was over, she took the steps down toward his podium to say hello. To not speak to him would be worse, she thought.

On her way down, Brian stopped her in the aisle.

"Hey," he said. "How's it going?"

"Great," she said. "How are you?"

"I've been better. My dog passed away this weekend. He was over fifteen years old and was the best dog I've ever known."

"Brian, I'm so sorry. Are you talking about Buck?"

Buck was a Jack Russel Terrier who'd been sweet as could be. She used to hold him in her lap when she'd watch movies with Brian at his place during their senior year of high school. Buck went camping with them at Enchanted Rock and fishing at Choke Canyon State Park. The dog used to love riding in Brian's jeep with his head hanging out of the passenger side window while Denise held him.

Brian nodded. "He was such a good boy. We got him when I was only six years old. I can barely remember life without him."

He wiped his face with the bottom of his t-shirt and sniffed.

She gave him a hug. "I'm sorry, Brian. I know how much you loved Buck, and how much he loved you."

"Thanks," he said. "Well, I just thought you'd want to know. I'll catch you later."

She watched Brian climb up the remaining steps to the back exit before she turned back toward Markos. He was waiting for her with a pained expression on his face.

"Markos?" she asked. "What's wrong?"

"Could you come by my office after your next class? I need to talk to you."

"Of course. Everything okay?" Was he breaking up with her before they'd even started?

"I just have something I need to get off my chest."

His reply certainly didn't make the situation less mysterious.

"Okay," she said. "I'll see you in an hour."

Denise could barely focus during her composition class, and when the period finally ended, it was with dread in her heart that she headed across campus to Markos's office.

As usual, his door was ajar, and she saw him behind his desk, looking at the electronic cube she had seen him with last time, consternation once again on his face.

She tapped on the door. "Markos?"

He put away the device and stood up. "Denise." He made his way around his desk and hugged her. "We need to have a difficult conversation."

"Why? What's wrong?"

"Sit down," he said.

Denise felt as if she were floating out of her body. Her body was numb, and the experience was surreal, as if she were in the moment and not in the moment at the same time. She sat on the chair, but she felt as though she were still standing. She stared at a painting across the room, and she saw it and didn't see it.

Markos pulled his desk chair closer to her. "I care so much about you, Denise. I really do."

Still in the fog, she said, "But?"

"I need you to hear my life story before we go any further with this."

"Okay. I'm listening." But she was surrounded by fog and could barely hear him.

"Not here. I want to take you to my yacht. There's something I need to show you."

She blinked, clearing away the haze. "When?"

"I'm obligated to teach one more semester," he said. "But we can go over Spring Break."

"That's months away. Are you saying I have to wait that long to hear your story?"

He took her hands in his and leaned close to her. "Listen to me, Denise. There was a time when I believed that Mariela was the love of my life. But in spending these last few months with you, I've come to believe…" He cleared his throat. "Oh, Denise, I honestly believe that *you* could be the love of my life."

Her mouth dropped open as she searched his eyes, the haze around her finally clearing. "Markos, I…"

"But you must hear my story before we allow ourselves to go further," he insisted. "I need to know that you can accept me and everything I've done, even though I've finally come to realize that you have always been a part of it. You, Denise. You have been the one constant in all of this."

She bent her brows. "How? I don't understand."

"I know you don't. But you will. And hopefully, once you hear everything, we can be together."

When he didn't lean in and kiss her, she frowned. Spring Break had never seemed so far away.

CHAPTER EIGHT

Second Kiss

Denise thought it was probably a good thing that she and Markos didn't see each other during final exams, because it helped her to focus on studying and writing her final essay. And she was extremely proud of herself when she received her grades and learned she'd made an A in every one of her classes.

But once exams were over and the semester had come to an end and she was no longer seeing Markos at school, Denise began to feel blue. And as the Christmas holidays neared, her family wanted to know if Markos was coming. She put off answering them at Sunday dinner, but when her father asked again a few days before Christmas, she decided to call Markos and invite him. Surely, he'd rather be there with them than spending Christmas alone.

She stared at her phone, screwing up the courage, as she practiced ways she would deliver her invitation.

Practice One: *Hello, Markos. I was just calling to see if you'd like to come to Christmas dinner. My family and I would like to see you.*

Practice Two: *Hello, Markos. I'm sorry to bother you, but my family insists that I invite you for Christmas dinner.*

Practice Three: *Hi, Markos. If you're not doing anything on Christmas day, why don't you join me and my family for dinner? I'm baking my famous lemon cream cake.*

She took a deep breath and punched in his number, still not sure what she would say.

When he answered, he said, "Denise! I'm so glad you called. I just returned from another trip, and I brought you a gift. Mind if I come by and give it to you?"

"Sure! I'd love that!" she replied, a little too eagerly. "When?"

"Is now a bad time?" he asked.

"Not at all. Come on over!"

When she ended the call, she squealed, and her father came running from his room.

"Everything okay?" he asked, when he saw her on the sofa, smiling.

"It is *now*, Daddy!"

An hour later, Markos knocked on Denise's front door. She had showered and changed into a cute sweater and jeans, wanting to look her best for this opportunity to remind Markos of his attraction to her. After she took his coat and hung it in the front closet, they sat together on the sofa. She'd already given her father strict instructions to stay in his room unless told otherwise, so she and Markos could be alone. Her father had been happy to comply.

Once they were seated side by side, Markos pulled a small box wrapped in gold and white wrapping paper from his trouser pocket. It was the same size box in which one would expect to find an engagement ring.

Denise stifled a gasp. There was no way he'd propose after what he'd said about her needing to hear his story. Was there?

"Here's my Christmas present to you." He handed her the box. "I hope you like it."

"You've already given me the best present you could," she said as she clutched the sapphire pendant at her breast.

"This gift is more practical, less sentimental, than that one."

She took a deep breath. Then it wasn't an engagement ring. She was both relieved and disappointed, but she knew she'd love anything Markos gave to her. She tore off the gold and white wrapping and unhinged the wooden box to find something resembling a digital watch. It had a sparkling wrist band made of white gold, just like the chain that held her sapphire pendant. Along the two-inch-by-two-inch digital screen were tiny diamonds. A white gold charm, resembling a teacher's pointer, hung on a small chain from the diamond trim.

"Is this a watch?" she asked. "It's beautiful."

"So much more than a watch," he said. "It's like a smart phone, with internet access and interchangeable solar powered batteries." He lifted the silky fabric that lined the bottom of the box to show two thin plastic panels. "You place these solar batteries near a window to charge all day, and then you swap the one back here out when needed. Each battery will usually last about a week. I make a habit of changing mine out on the weekend. Works like a charm."

He showed her the band on his wrist. His band was made of dark brown leather, and the screen was trimmed with a thin band of gold. She'd never seen him wear it before, or else it was hidden beneath the cuff of his sleeve. Like hers, his watch had a charm, but his was yellow gold.

"What do the charms represent?" she asked.

"Those are styluses," he said, using his against the touch screen on the face of the watch. "See? It's easier than using your fingertips. Much more efficient."

"I didn't even know that technology like this existed," she said. "Thank you so much."

He helped her put it on. "It's not yet available to the public, but, like I told you, I have connections. I picked this one up at one of my labs abroad especially for you."

"How thoughtful of you, Markos. I can't thank you enough."

"It's my pleasure. I'm glad you like it. It can do anything a computer can do, and it comes with hundreds of apps already built in. You'll be amazed by all the things this device can do. It's more than a phone, more than a computer. I'd love to show you some of the features, if you have time."

"I always have time for you," she said with a smile. "But before you do, there's something I wanted to ask you. It's actually why I called you earlier. My family and I were hoping you'd join us here for Christmas dinner. We celebrate in the evening on Christmas Eve. Can you come?"

He glanced down at his hands. "I really wish I could. I would love nothing more. But the holidays offer me the only opportunity until next summer to do the extensive traveling required of some of my most important work. I hope you understand."

Denise had expected him to accept. She was surprised and devastated. "When do you leave?"

"In the morning. I'm sorry, Denise. Please don't be sad." He lifted her chin and gazed down at her with his stunning emerald eyes. "Once you hear my story, if you still feel about me the way you do now, you can come with me on my travels. I'd love to introduce you to my work. In a way, you were the one who started me on this journey."

"You said something like that before. What do you mean?" she asked.

"You'll understand once you hear my story. For now, can you be patient?"

"Why can't you tell me your story tonight?" she asked.

"Because there's something I need to show you for you to fully understand. Will you trust me?"

She nodded, wanting so badly to be kissed and held by him again.

He must have read her mind, because he said, "I was hoping my travels would keep you off my mind, that I'd be too busy saving the world to think about the other night and how badly I wish for more nights like it."

"And has it worked?' she asked mischievously.

He gave her a wide grin. "Not in the least."

Flushed with heat and longing, she took another deep breath, feeling as though she couldn't breathe. "Oh, Markos."

He was still holding her chin with one finger as he gazed into her eyes. Then he glanced down at her body, as if her were drinking in her image. Denise felt a pulse of desire move between her legs.

"Maybe once more," he half-whispered, half-growled as he covered her lips with his.

He crushed her body against his, a moan escaping his throat. Denise closed her eyes and moved her hands over his muscled arms and back, and pressed even closer, closer against him. She was falling into a state of ecstasy, forgetting time and place, forgetting where she was, who she was.

"Markos."

As soon as she'd said his name, he pulled away. "I'm sorry."

"Don't be," she said, breathless.

"You need to hear everything first. You need to know what it is you're getting into with me. It's not fair to you otherwise." He stood up. "I'm sorry, Denise, but I better go. I'd give anything to stay." He hastened to the closet for his coat. "Please tell your family I said, 'Merry Christmas,' will you?"

She nodded as he slipped into his coat and left.

CHAPTER NINE

Third Kiss

Over the next several weeks, Denise was plagued with doubts. She began to worry that Professor Markos Nadir was playing her for a fool. He was a wealthy man—he owned a yacht and traveled the world. Perhaps he gave expensive gifts to unsuspecting college girls and made them fall in love with him by seducing them with his mysterious ways. Maybe Denise wasn't special. How could he possibly tell her she could be the love of his life after knowing her for only four months? Had she been a sucker?

She kept herself busy braiding, cutting, and coloring hair and venting to her clients. "What should I do?" she'd ask each one after explaining her strange situation with Markos Nadir.

Lucinda told her to chill and stop being so paranoid.

Celeste told her to demand to hear the man's life story before agreeing to go on the trip. "It could be a trap."

Bethany told her to ask Markos if Bethany could go on the yacht with them. "I'll watch your back."

Andre told her that no dude would avoid being with her for *any* reason and there must be something wrong with Markos.

On New Year's Eve, Brian invited Denise to a house party his fraternity was hosting. Since she had nothing else to do but wonder about Markos, and since it didn't sound like Brian was asking her to be his date, Denise said she would go if she could bring Lucinda, who had complained that she had nothing to do.

Denise wasn't old enough to drink, and she'd promised Lucinda she'd be the designated driver, and other than Brian and Lucinda, she knew no one there. Consequently, she was bored and wishing she was with Markos.

Just before the countdown to 2018, as Denise stood in a crowded room surrounded by a haze of cigarette smoke and the pungent smell of beer, Brian came up beside her and asked her if she and their professor were a thing.

"What? No," she lied.

"I've noticed the way he looks at you and you him," Brian said.

"We're not a thing," Denise insisted.

Lucinda, who was drunk and within earshot, called out, "Don't lie, girlfriend!"

"I don't know what we are," Denise said truthfully. "He's been avoiding me."

"So, you *were* a thing?" he said.

Denise shrugged. "Why does it matter?"

Brian gave her a hurt look. "I guess it doesn't."

He walked off to get another beer from the keg.

A few minutes later, Denise was surprised when Brian returned after the countdown to give her a New Year's kiss—on the lips!

"Brian," she complained, but with a smile and not before he had finished his kiss. "You and I are not a thing, okay?"

"I know, but there was no reason not to ring in the new year together, right?"

"Right." And there was no reason to make him feel bad about it, so she smiled, talked with him about school, and then, about thirty minutes later, told Lucinda it was time to go.

Denise was anxious to begin the spring semester—not because she was ready to dive into her studies again, but because she was hoping to run into Markos. He was teaching the same class he had taught in the fall, so she had a different physics professor, which was probably better for her learning if not for her heart. On the first day of class, she walked by his office and glanced toward his door—ajar as usual—and caught a peek of him sitting behind his desk talking to another student—a girl about Denise's age. Denise stood outside the door to listen.

She dreaded the possibility of overhearing him saying the same things to the student inside his office that he had said to Denise, and relief swept over her when that didn't happen. He and the student spoke solely of vectors and graphs and of nothing as interesting as reverse magnetism, gravitational lensing, and the shimmering effect.

Denise had become so distracted by the sound of Markos's deep and alluring voice that she had ceased to hear *what* he was saying and was caught off guard when the student was suddenly exiting through his door. Not wanting to be seen eavesdropping, Denise ran, as fast as she could, down the hall, past the elevator, to the stairwell. Once she was safely outside of the building she caught her breath.

In the month of February, Denise's father enrolled in a teacher certification course through a program at Region 20, a multi-district educational facility. Before his honorable discharge, her father had been a lab technician in the military, so it seemed only natural that he should choose to become a high school biology teacher. The program would take one year to complete, not including another six months of student teaching. Denise was thrilled that her father would finally be getting out of the house. First, he needed to retake his driving test, because he'd let his license expire.

Between helping her father study for his driving test, helping him fill out the application for the teaching certification class, cooking their dinners, working at the salon, attending classes, and keeping up with her studies, Denise should have had no time to think about Markos. But Denise did think about him. She thought about him every minute of every day, even while she was doing other things.

She managed to stay away from him and avoided calling or texting until one day, near the end of February. She had to see him. She crept down the hall toward his office and saw his door ajar. She quietly stood beside it and, when she didn't hear him talking to a student, she edged around to the other side of the door to have a peek.

His office was empty.

Just then, he emerged down the hallway from the men's room. He noticed her immediately, so it would do no good to run away this time.

"Denise!" he cried when he was still only halfway between one end of the hall and her.

She waited for him to catch up with her, unable to think of a word to say.

When he reached her, he embraced her and kissed her on the cheek. Before pulling away, he whispered, "I've been in agony. It's so good to see you."

"Hello, Markos." She felt awkward and nervous but elated to see him. "I've missed you."

"Can you come inside for a moment?" he asked.

She followed him into his office. As soon as he'd closed the door behind her, he took her into his arms.

"I've thought of nothing but you," he said in between kisses.

"Same," she whispered, barely able to speak, as she kissed him back.

His breath was sweet and hot against her lips. She felt like she was in a dream, unable to believe this was really happening.

"So why haven't you called?" she finally managed to say.

"You know why," he kissed her neck.

She felt a pulse of desire between her legs. "Are we still on for Spring Break, or have our plans changed?"

He stopped to look at her. "Those plans haven't changed. You're still going with me, aren't you? I'm anxious to tell you my story."

"Can't you begin your story now and finish it on the yacht?" she asked.

He turned his face toward the ceiling, pondering the idea. "Maybe that's not a bad idea. Not now, but over dinner."

"When?"

"Friday night," he said. "Then we'll leave for my yacht the following Friday."

A mixture of relief and anxiety washed over her. She was relieved that he seemed as devoted to her as he'd been before Christmas, but she was anxious to learn why he couldn't be with her until after he divulged the details of his life. What had he done that made him skeptical of her ability to accept him?

Friday night, Markos arrived at her house to pick her up for their date. He hugged her at the door and then entered the living room and shook her father's hand.

"It's been a long time since we've seen you around here," her father said with less affection than he had shown at Thanksgiving.

"My apologies, Mr. Walker," Markos said. "I've been traveling for my work and tied up with lectures, but things are about to change now that Spring Break is around the corner."

"And where exactly is it that you intend to take my daughter?" Denise's father asked.

"Tonight, we're going to Frank's Steakhouse," Markos said, "but I suspect what you really want to know is where I plan to take her in March."

"That's right," her father said.

Markos cleared his throat—a nervous habit Denise had come to recognize. "We'll fly to Guam, where I keep my yacht. From there it's a few hours' trip to the Mariana Trench—the deepest known part of any ocean on Earth."

Her father's eyes darkened. "You're going on a boat?"

"He's going to teach me to scuba dive," Denise said. "I'm so excited. I've always wanted to learn."

"I'm a licensed sea captain with over three years of experience," Markos added. "Your daughter will be safe in my care. I promise."

Her father sighed. "I have no right to deny her. She's a grown woman. Independent. She's taken care of me all these years."

Denise put her arms around her father. "I promise to be careful, Daddy. Okay?"

"I know you will, Baby, but it's my job to worry."

At the restaurant, Markos seemed less talkative than he had been in his office—less affectionate, too. Denise felt like she was riding a roller coaster, but instead of enjoying a thrilling ride, she was sick from the ups and downs.

"The food is delicious," she said, even though her nerves were making her stomach queasy.

"You've barely taken two bites," he pointed out.

"Because I'm anxious to hear your story," she said.

"About that." Markos took a quick sip of water. "Every time I try to think of where to begin, I realize that there's nothing I can say that will make any sense without you first seeing what I need you to see with your own eyes."

"Have a little faith in me." This was getting old. If he didn't start talking, she was going to start walking.

"I have more faith in you than you can imagine," he said. "Alright, then. Let's see. Let me go back, to how I ended up here in the first place."

"That sounds like a good place to start." She took a bite of her steak. Now that he was talking, her stomach settled.

"When I was in high school my parents decided to move from New York City to a small town in Indiana."

"Oh? When did they decide to move back to New York?"

"That's another story," he said. "Let's stick with this one, okay?"

"Okay." Denise felt as if he'd just scolded her, and she quickly took a sip of her iced tea to hide her embarrassment.

"I did my undergraduate studies at a university not far from where we lived but decided to attend medical school in Baylor, Texas."

"How long ago was that?" Denise asked.

"I started med school when I was almost twenty-one. I was doing an internship in San Antonio when I met Mariela a few years later. She had just turned twenty."

"The age I am now."

"Yes," he said. "We were married within the year."

"How did you meet?" Denise asked, wanting and not wanting to know the details.

"A new club had opened up over where the old Trader Joe's used to be in Quarry Village," he said.

"I didn't realize Trader Joe's was originally in a different location from where it is now," Denise said.

"Anyway, that's not important," Markos said. "I had gone for a beer after my shift with a few coworkers, and Mariela was there, sitting all by herself. I dared one of my friends to invite her to join us, and she did."

"Why didn't you invite her yourself?" Denise teased.

"I was young and foolish."

"But older than I am now," Denise pointed out.

"You are wise beyond your years," he said.

"Anyway," she said. "What happened next?"

"My friend and I both liked Mariela, but she preferred me. All night, he kept fighting me for her attention. It turned out she wasn't alone. She had come with two friends, who'd been out on the dance floor. So, my friend, Jack, eventually gave up on Mariela and started moving in on her friend, Katrina. They spent the night dancing together."

"You weren't a dancer?" Denise asked.

"I preferred conversation," he said. "I wanted to know everything about Mariela."

Denise hid her feelings of jealousy as she realized that he hadn't seemed to want to know everything about *her*.

"When the club closed," Markos continued. "Mariela said we should go swimming."

"Swimming? What time was it?"

"Two in the morning," he said. "But none of us were ready for the night to end, so I invited everyone over to my apartment, and we went skinny dipping in the pool."

Denise laughed, imagining Markos being drunk and silly and naked. "That sounds hilarious."

"We had a great time until the security guard kicked us out and threatened to call the police."

Denise laughed again.

"You should have seen us clamoring for our clothes—we hadn't thought to bring towels—and streaking across the parking lot to my apartment."

"I can imagine."

"I made coffee for everyone, and, once the girls were sober, they went home, but not without giving us their numbers. I called Mariela the very next day to ask her out again, and she said yes."

"Just the two of you?"

"Like I said, I preferred conversation."

"Tell me more about Mariela. Was she a student when you met, or was she already working?"

"She was a student at a local university—a finance major. She was training to become an investment broker at her father's firm."

"My brother's an investment broker," Denise pointed out. "He does pretty well, though it didn't start out so great for him. He helped build the company into what it is today, and he couldn't have done it without Kassia's financial support."

"Mariela was lucky that her parents paved the way for her success," Markos said. "A year after we met, we were married, but the diagnosis came within two months of that, and she died just before our first anniversary."

Two years ago, Denise realized. "I'm so sorry."

He reached across the table and squeezed her hand. "This is going to sound strange, but, in a way, what happened in my past has led me to you."

She lifted her brows. "That's so sweet."

He lowered his voice and leaned across the table, still holding her hand. "I didn't used to believe in fate, or in the idea that things happened for a reason, but over the past two years, my philosophy has changed. I think that you and I are soulmates and that we've been on a journey together for much longer than either of us realize."

CHAPTER TEN

First Day at Sea

A week later, Denise could hardly contain her excitement when Markos arrived at her house to pick her up.

He took her in his arms as soon as she had answered the door and asked, "Are you ready for the adventure of your life?"

She grinned up at him. "Ready."

The flight from San Antonio to Los Angeles was uneventful, but the one from LA to Honolulu was made interesting by a set of twins—girls aged four—in the seats in front of them. Having nothing better to do, the girls played peek-a-boo on and off throughout the six-hour flight. They were adorable at first, but, toward the end of the trip, Denise wanted to throw something at them to knock them unconscious.

During their layover in Honolulu, Markos bought Denise a beautiful lei of Pikaka—or Arabian Jasmine. The tiny fragrant blossoms formed a delicate strand, resembling pearls. Then she and Markos ate an evening dinner of lau lau, kalua pork, lomi lomi salmon, poi, haupia, and rice at a restaurant in the airport. Denise had never eaten anything like it before. As much as she enjoyed trying something new, she preferred the Mexican food in San Antonio to Hawaiian cuisine.

Using the digital wristlet Markos had given her for Christmas, Denise texted her father each time they'd landed safely. Once, someone sitting next to her in the airport asked her about the device, and she had to explain that it wasn't yet out on the market.

On the flight to Guam, Denise snuggled against Markos beneath a blanket. She felt safe in his arms—and content. She didn't mind the long flight while she was lying against him. She soon fell asleep and didn't awaken until the wheels hit the landing strip at Guam International Airport in the early morning.

Before boarding the yacht, Markos needed to pick up some supplies in town—mainly fresh food. He said he had plenty of canned and jarred items, but he wanted to treat her to better food than he usually ate when sailing alone. They took a cab to the market not far from Apra Harbor.

It should have been no surprise to Denise that Markos's ship was named *The Mariela*. It was a three-tiered vessel with two masts. Once they boarded, they unloaded their supplies on the deck, and then he took her to the lowest level in the hull of the ship to the cabins, so they could put away their bags.

The hull had three cabins. Markos's room was located in the front of the ship, in what Markos referred to as the bow, and Denise's was down the corridor, past a laundry facility and engineering room, in the back side, in one of two cabins located in the back of the ship, in what Markos referred to as the stern. Her cabin was small but comfortable with a full bed, closet, and private bath. The shower was tiny, but it would serve its purpose. Above the bed was a portal to the sea—Denise's favorite part of the room. She leaned closer for a better view and saw what she thought might be a manatee—or else a very fat fish without scales—but it was gone from her view as fast as it had come into it.

Denise was disappointed that she and Markos wouldn't be sharing a cabin. She had assumed that they would be sleeping together. He probably wanted her to hear his story before inviting her to share his bed. She hoped he would tell it to her tonight. The anxiety was killing her.

From the hull of the ship, Markos led her up to the next level of the yacht. In the back was a deck, where they had stashed the bags of groceries. This deck had a table and bench, covered by the deck above. From this lower deck, she and Marcos carried the supplies through the salon—which was nicely furnished with a sofa, two club chairs, and a flat-screen television—to the kitchen, where Markos quickly put away the fresh fruits, vegetables, meats, and bread. In the front of the ship was a square table surrounded on three sides by a u-shaped bench. A large window gave a beautiful view to the front, where there was another deck and mast. Steps from the kitchen led to that front deck, and even more led to the uppermost level where the cockpit was, surrounded by glass on three sides. There were two leather seats and a control panel, and behind it was the upper deck with a long couch, facing the back of the ship.

"It's incredible," Denise said for the third time since they had begun the tour.

"I'm glad you like it," he said. "I know you must be tired from the trip, so if you'd like to rest while I get us out to sea, please be my guest."

"Are you kidding? I'm too excited to rest. I want to see you doing your thing!"

He threw his head back and laughed. "Good. Then you can help. But first, let's get changed, shall we?"

He led her back down to the hull of the ship to their cabins. Behind closed doors, she changed from her jeans into her bikini, which she covered with cute shorts and a tank top. To deal with the winds, she tied her hair in a ponytail. Then, after finding her sunglasses, she removed her sapphire pendant and digital wristlet and headed back to the front deck, where Markos was already preparing the sails.

Denise gasped when she saw him in nothing but shorts and sandals. His chiseled back and chest were breathtaking beneath the bright sun, even nicer looking than she'd imagined. She couldn't believe he was in love with her and that there was a chance they could be together forever. It seemed like a dream.

"Well, aren't you adorable?" he said when he noticed her on deck.

"I could say the same of you," she said laughing—though, 'adorable' wasn't exactly the word she was thinking of.

"Then, why don't you?"

"Well, aren't you adorable!"

They both laughed.

She tried her best to help with the rigging before Markos launched the boat from the dock and headed for the open sea. As she sat beside him in the cockpit, she observed all the activity around them. There were other vessels making their way in and out of the harbor, so it was slow sailing until they made it past the first small island. With the sun showering its rays down on the sea from up in the eastern sky ahead of them, the calm waters sparkled like crystal, inviting them onward. The breeze was swift but refreshing. The temperature was neither too hot nor too cold. Denise felt exhilarated and couldn't recall ever feeling happier than she was at this moment.

By lunchtime, they had reached the spot where Markos wanted to anchor. Although there had been dozens of ships in and around the harbor, *The Mariela* was alone, except for what appeared to be a fishing boat in the distance.

Denise and Markos returned to the kitchen and made sandwiches and salads.

While they ate at the table by the picture window overlooking the ship's bow, Denise said, "So, tell me more about the Mariana Trench. Why are we here?"

"It's the deepest point of the ocean floor," he said. "It's even deeper than Mount Everest is tall."

"Right below us?" It was scary to think of the deep abyss.

"Just west of here," he said. "About a mile away. This is the closest place to anchor the boat."

"Why is it so deep there?" she asked.

"It's where two tectonic plates collide with each other, forcing one deeper into the mantle."

"So, it's getting deeper over time?"

"Maybe a millimeter per year."

"Are there are a lot of earthquakes in this area?"

"I would imagine so," he said, before taking the last bite of his sandwich.

"How long will it take us to swim that far down?" she asked, feeling intimidated by the sheer idea of Mount Everest's proportions.

"Our bodies couldn't handle the pressure," he said. "The only way we can get there is by submarine."

"But, Markos, this ship isn't a sub. I don't understand."

"No, but it contains one." He gave her a wink.

"Where? Are you teasing me?"

"There's a small vessel in the engineering room below." His eyes twinkled.

"But you said we'd be diving. Isn't that why you're teaching me?"

"Once we get to the other side, we'll have to anchor the vessel and swim to port."

"The other side of what?"

"Of the trench."

She laughed. He must be joking. "Right. So, when do we start?"

"As soon as you're ready."

"I'm ready!"

They put away their dishes and headed to the back deck. He lifted the cushions of the bench to reveal scuba gear. She tore off her clothes down to her bikini and blushed when she noticed Markos checking her out. He helped her into a wetsuit.

"Damn, you're cute," he said, zipping her in.

She laughed. "What about you? Aren't you going to wear a wet suit, too?"

"First, we're going to go over everything here, on the deck. I may let you do a shallow dive, just to get a feel, alright? I want you to be safe."

Denise nodded. "Yes, Captain."

"Alright, then," he said with a chuckle. "Are you familiar with how to wear a mask?"

He taught her a few things she didn't know—like how to get a good fit and how to keep it from fogging up.

"This is your BCD—Buoyancy Control Device." He slipped a vest on her and zipped it over her wet suit. "You need to know how to maintain your buoyancy so you can control how deep you want to be."

"Why is it so heavy?"

"It's full of lead weights." He unzipped a pocket near her left breast.

Her nipple hardened beneath the suit, and she bit her lip. She took a deep breath as she noticed the way his curly hair had flattened in the wind around his face, framing his emerald eyes. He was so beautiful.

Next, he brought out a tube with a mouthpiece on one end. "This is your regulator. It will deliver air on demand at just the right pressure. This end goes in your mouth, and this end will attach to the tank. This other piece connects to your BCD, so it can fill up little bladders of air when you want to float higher, or it can draw air out of the vest when you want to sink lower." He showed her another gadget. "This is your SPG—your pressure gauge. It lets you know how much air you have in the tank."

"Oh, that's important."

"Yes."

He helped her put the gear on as he taught her how to use each part, leaving the fins for last.

"We'll go for a very shallow dive, right here near the back of the boat," he said. "I'm going in snorkel gear—that's how shallow. Okay?"

She squealed. "This is exciting!"

He laughed at her. "You're too cute, Denise. I'm glad you aren't afraid."

"Oh, I'm plenty afraid! I'm just more excited than scared—that's all!"

"I'll be right beside you. And there's no need to worry about marine life. Shark attacks are very rare, okay?"

"Gee, I hadn't been thinking of sharks. Thanks a lot!"

He laughed again. "I wouldn't put you in danger. You *must* know that."

She nodded. "I trust you."

He helped her to the back of the boat and then demonstrated how she should fall back into the water.

When he re-emerged, looking wet and sexier than ever, she asked, "Is the water cold?"

"You better believe it! But you'll get used to it, okay?"

"Okay."

"Ready?"

"Ready!" Her heart was beating a million miles a minute—or at least that's how it felt. She couldn't believe she was about to dive for the very first time—even if it was a baby dive. "Here goes nothing!"

She plunged backward into the water and was engulfed by the cold, cold sea. She was surprised by how quickly she descended, deeper than the ship. A school of silver fish swam several yards below. She couldn't see the bottom of the ocean, but what she could see was so vast, so enormous! She felt like a speck of dust in comparison.

Just as she was about to panic, Markos was beside her, doing something to her vest. Pockets of air filled her BCD, and she began to rise. She realized she hadn't been breathing when Markos motioned for her to breathe in.

She was scared to breathe. What if it didn't work? What if she got lungs full of water? She quickly kicked and pulled her way back to the surface, ripped off the mouthpiece, and gulped in air.

Markos emerged right beside her. "What happened?"

"I guess I panicked."

He towed her to the boat. "That's okay. That's why we're practicing."

He helped her back onto the deck, where she caught her breath. Then, kneeling beside her, Markos told her to breathe with the regulator.

"Just see what it's like, and maybe you'll be less fearful about trying it underwater."

She gave it a try. It wasn't so bad, but would it still work when she was surrounded by water?

"Ready to try once more?" he asked.

"You won't let me drown?" she asked, realizing that diving was much more frightening than she had anticipated.

"I promise."

Trembling this time, she followed Markos to the edge of the boat and watched him fall into the sea. Then she positioned the mouthpiece between her lips, breathed from it to remind herself she could, and fell back.

A few hours later, after Denise had had a warm shower and a change of clothes—a yellow sundress and sandals she'd bought just for this trip— she met Markos in the salon for dinner. He was in the kitchen, wearing a peach button-down, short-sleeved shirt and khaki shorts and sandals. He hadn't buttoned the shirt, and his dark chest glistened in the low rays from the setting sun that came in through the picture window overlooking the bow. He was preparing fresh salmon, which he broiled in butter and lemon sauce, with bell pepper and onions.

He grinned at her as soon as she entered. "You look beautiful."

"I didn't know you could cook."

"I learned from the best," he said.

"Oh? And who was that?" she asked as he handed her a plate, and they made their way to the table.

"Um, my wife's aunt," he said, avoiding her eyes. "She was a great cook, like you."

There was a strange awkwardness between them as they sat across from one another. The view from the window was incredible as the sunset streaked the sky with pinks and purples.

Denise took a bite of the salmon. "Oh, wow."

"I'm glad you like it."

After a few more minutes of eating in silence, Denise's curiosity got the best of her. "So, tell me what drew you to Mariela. What was it about her that made you fall in love?"

He seemed caught off guard by the question.

"I'm sorry. You don't have to answer that," she said.

"No, it's okay," he said. "Hmm. Where do I begin?"

Denise regretted the question, not sure if she wanted the answer.

"I suppose I was first attracted by her beauty. I had never seen someone so stunning."

He must have noticed how uncomfortable she was because he added, "Until I met you, of course."

She gave him a smile that was half-forced, but she said nothing.

"I enjoyed how impulsive and spontaneous she was, which was the very opposite of me. Everything I do is calculating, from the big life-decisions, such as which career to pursue or which university to attend, all the way down to which loaf of bread to buy at the grocery store."

"And how would you describe me in that regard?" she asked.

"You, my dear, are the perfect combination of us both. You have Mariela's adventurous spirit, but it's tempered by an analytical mind that exceeds my own."

She laughed. "You can't possibly know that about me. We haven't spent enough time together."

"Do you disagree with my assessment?" he challenged.

She shook her head. He'd described her to a tee. But how?

"Since you don't seem to think I know you well enough, tell me more about you," Markos said.

"Let's take turns," she suggested. "Tell me something shocking about you."

"Ladies first."

Denise should have seen that coming. She took a sip of Coke and thought about what she could say. If she wanted Markos to open up and engage in a deeper conversation with her, she had to do the same.

"No one knows this about me," she said. Her lips twitched with anxiety. "But, when I was fifteen, I no longer believed that any of this mattered. My mother had died in a senseless accident when I was fourteen. My father rightfully blamed himself and wrongfully took it out on my brother. My brother wanted nothing to do with us and had moved out as soon as he could. And my life became about survival—mine and my father's."

Markos squeezed her hand. "I'm so sorry."

"I came to a point where I truly believed that my father and I would be better off dead." There, she'd said it. She wasn't sure why she was saying it, but it felt good to unburden herself. She avoided Markos's gaze as the blood rushed to her cheeks and time seemed to stop.

When she finally looked at him, Markos was frowning. He waited, patiently, for her to continue.

After a long moment, she said, "I couldn't bring myself to kill him, but I thought about it hundreds of times. I researched ways to do it. I even bought…" she stopped to catch her breath. "I bought poison and was going to put it in his stew."

Tears streamed down her cheeks and a sob choked her in the back of her throat. She coughed and covered her face.

"My poor, sweet, Denise. It's okay." He reached across the table and wiped her tears with his thumb. "It's okay."

"I couldn't do it," she said again. "But I thought that if I took my own life, he'd probably follow, and, if he didn't, well, it wouldn't be my problem anymore."

The guilt and the hate built up inside of her. She'd never admitted it before. She *couldn't* admit it before. But she had hated her father. She had *hated* him!

She broke into ugly sobs, her entire body convulsing. Markos stood up and pulled her to her feet and into his arms, holding her around her waist. "It's okay," he said again.

"I took my father's pistol," she managed to say. "I keep it in my room now. I've lost count of how many times I've taken it with me to the bathroom, held it to my temple, ready to pull the trigger."

"I didn't know," Markos said. "I had no idea. I'm so, so sorry. Oh, Denise."

He held her close against him as he kissed her temple—the very temple where she had pressed the barrel of the gun.

She collapsed against him.

"Listen to me," he whispered. "You're an amazing woman who has been through so much in her young life already. Don't judge yourself so harshly."

"I know, but…"

"The fact is, you *didn't* kill your father. You saved his life. And you *didn't* kill yourself. You saved *mine*. You don't know it yet, but, sweet, sweet Denise, you saved my life!"

She tightened her arms around his neck and pressed against him, grateful to finally have someone who could bear this horrible, ugly side of her and still love her. As the tears flowed down her cheeks, she felt free—finally free of the hate and the guilt and the loss.

"You saved *mine*," she whispered back, "by helping my father, and by loving me. Markos, you saved *mine*."

With a passionate grip, he cupped her face and pressed his lips hard against hers. Emotions beyond anything she'd ever felt engulfed her. She held on to Markos, pressed herself against Markos, and loved Markos.

He swept her up in his arms and carried her to the long couch on the upper deck, where he laid her on her back. The sun had long disappeared beneath the horizon, and they were bathed in moonlight. Gently, but passionately, he peeled away her clothes, and then he helped her peel away his. She gasped at the sight of his magnificent body and yield-ed to every pleasure it gave her.

They loved each other on the magnificent yacht on the big, wide sea beneath the enormous starry sky. They loved each other totally and completely. Afterward, as she lay in his arms, Denise believed that may-be life could have meaning and purpose. Maybe her purpose was to love Markos.

CHAPTER ELEVEN

Second Day at Sea

Denise and Markos fell asleep side by side on the couch of the upper deck beneath the enormous sky. When the light of the early dawn awakened her, along with the sounds of gentle waves and of distant seagulls, Denise opened her eyes to find Markos still lying beside her, holding her in his arms.

"I didn't want to wake you," he said. "Did you sleep well?"

"I think that was the best sleep I've had in years." She smiled up at him.

He kissed her on the cheek. "Hungry?"

"Not yet." She gazed up at blue sky and felt the light breeze against her skin. The company, the setting, the way she felt in her heart—it couldn't get any better than this.

"When are we diving?" she asked, eager to get started.

"Whenever you're ready." He kissed her nose.

"Let me brush my teeth and change. Then I'll be ready."

"I'll meet you on the lower deck."

When she returned in her bikini, she found him bent over the oxygen tank in his swim trunks. She studied his muscled back and arms and sighed, recalling how incredible she had felt while lying beside him. He turned and caught her watching him. He lifted a brow with amusement.

She covered her blush and said, "Busted. Sorry!"

He stood up and wrapped his arms around her. "Don't apologize. I'm glad you want me as much as I want you."

She met his lips with her own. Heaven could not possibly be better than this, she thought.

Once they were both fitted with their gear, they dropped into the cold sea. She focused on her breathing, still fearful of taking in water. She normally breathed through her nose, so it took great concentration for her to breathe through her mouth.

The light beneath the sea was brighter this morning than it had been the day before—whether because the sun was still rising, or because the sky was clearer, Denise didn't know. Whatever the reason, she could see further out, and she was amazed by the variety of marine life and its glorious colors.

Markos led her about fifty feet down. It was not far enough to see the ocean floor. The deep expanse that stretched on in darkness for miles and miles was haunting. Her head felt the pinch of the pressure, and she was glad when he led her back to the surface and onto the deck of the boat.

"I think you're ready for the SEABOB," he said.

"The what?"

"It's like a motorized kickboard," he explained. "It will help us go deeper and move faster through the water."

"Sounds fun!" she said.

It did sound fun until she discovered that they would each have to operate their own SEABOB, and she wouldn't be riding along with him. There were two of them—one yellow and the other red. They were about the size of a suitcase, but rounded, like the body of a dolphin with handles where the dolphin's eyes would be.

Markos lowered the SEABOBs into the water from the back of the boat. He'd been right to compare them to kickboards, in that the rider held onto the handles and the rest of the body dragged behind the SEABOB.

In between each handle, where the dorsal fin of a dolphin would be, was a dashboard. She didn't relish the idea of having to operate it on her own.

"You can do it," he said when he noticed her hesitation. "Just follow me."

First, he showed her how to operate it above water, like a mini jet ski.

"This is amazing!" she shouted over the sound of the motor as she sped across the surface of the sea with her body dragging behind her.

The feel of her body moving effortlessly through the water beneath the beautiful sky surrounded by nothing but lovely sparkling green waves made her feel like she was a dolphin or a mermaid—or some other creature altogether—in a magical world.

She practiced maneuvering in circles, following behind Markos. Then, when he stopped near the yacht, she pulled up beside him.

"This is so fun, Markos! I love it!"

"Watch this." Markos fit his regulator into his mouth, pushed the submerge button on the SEABOB dashboard, and disappeared.

Denise popped the regulator between her lips, breathed in the oxygen, and then maneuvered the SEABOB beneath the surface.

She slowly submerged, searching for Markos. When she couldn't see him in any direction, she bit down the panic and went deeper.

She was surprised when the rocky bottom of the sea came into view, and all along it were beautiful, colorful living things. A long, winding, spotted eel combed the nooks and crannies for food. A small gray octopus seemed to be excavating with all eight tentacles, pulling up pieces of rock and dropping them again. A school of silver fish swam away, revealing tiny crabs on the rocky floor where colorful tendrils sprouted. Denise wasn't sure if the tendrils were plant or animal, but they were beautiful. Then a gang of pufferfish arrived. Denise was amazed.

She almost didn't notice Markos pull up alongside her, and she wondered how long he'd been there, so close to her. He gave her a thumb's up, and she mimicked the gesture back to him.

Later, over a lunch of sandwiches and salad, after they'd showered and changed into fresh clothes, she said, "Thank you for today. It was absolutely breathtaking. I've never had so much fun."

"It *was* fun, wasn't it?" he said before taking a bite of his sandwich.

"The ocean is even more amazing than I imagined. It's so busy with life—with incredible, beautiful life!"

Markos said, "I think you're ready to hear the rest of my story."

She dipped the end of a celery stalk in salad dressing and took a bite. "I'm listening!"

He clenched his jaw and took a deep breath. Resting his elbows on the table, he squeezed his hands together, as if trying to get the last juice out of an already squeezed lemon.

"Markos?"

"This isn't as easy as I thought it would be."

She reached over and patted his thigh. "It's okay. Take your time."

"When Mariela got the diagnosis, I felt as if the ground had fallen out from underneath me," he began.

Denise frowned. "I can imagine." That's how she had felt when her mother had passed.

"I couldn't accept it," he said. "Until then, our lives had been perfect, and I couldn't accept that in a matter of months, it would all be over."

"Were you able to get help?" she asked.

"Yes." He smiled. "Mariela's aunt was a brilliant physicist."

"Was?"

"Is…was…anyway, she helped me come up with a plan."

"What kind of plan?"

"The idea was to bend back the fabric of space-time."

Denise narrowed her eyes. "That's not funny, Markos. Be serious."

"I am deadly serious."

"Are you saying her aunt wanted you to time travel?"

"Exactly. She wanted me—or one of us—to go back so that we could get Mariela to a doctor *earlier*, so the cancer could be detected in time to be treated. But *I* wanted to go forward in time, to find a cure and bring it back."

"Markos, I," Denise felt a chill scurry down her back, and for the first time since meeting him, she began to worry that the death of his wife had taken a much greater toll on him than she had realized. She studied his emerald eyes. "Are you telling me that you contemplated time travel?"

"I wouldn't have thought of it if Mariela's aunt hadn't shown me the possibility."

Denise was at a loss as to what to believe. "How? What did she do?"

"Remember. *I* was the doctor. *She* was the physicist. This was all *her* master plan, okay?"

"Okay. But I still don't get how."

"First, she calculated the most vulnerable places in space-time," he said.

"What do you mean *vulnerable*?"

"Places where the fabric of space-time could be manipulated."

"How?"

"Don't you remember what I taught you? Energy. An explosion of energy."

She narrowed her eyes. "Sounds dangerous."

"That's exactly why we turned to the sea, because the sheer amount of energy we needed to generate could devastate an entire city. And the underwater pressure could better contain the explosion and its resulting radiation."

She studied his face, how excited he'd become.

"At first, Mariela's aunt thought we should go to the Arctic Ocean and take advantage of the increased magnetism near the North Pole, but the frozen water proved to be too hazardous."

"You and Mariela's aunt actually created an explosion in the Arctic Sea?" Denise asked.

"No. We chartered a boat and immediately realized that, even in the summer months, the threat of ice bergs to us and to the environment created too great a risk. That's when she considered tectonic plates."

Denise watched him with skepticism. He was beautiful. She wanted to believe him, but her heart was breaking in two. She should have known it was too good to be true.

"We came here, to the Mariana Trench. She borrowed the submarine from NASA. She worked there, in Houston."

"How could she *borrow* a submarine?"

"For research. She helped build it. They trusted her, as did I."

Denise leaned forward, suspending her disbelief. Maybe he was telling the truth. She didn't believe his attempts at time travel could have been successful, but maybe that wasn't what he was trying to tell her. "Okay. Then what happened?"

"After a few exploratory missions, we chose a date. She stayed on the yacht while I took the sub and the nuclear explosive to the deepest point of the trench. We argued over who would go, and, in the end, I won."

Denise put her hand to her mouth. "But you didn't detonate the explosive, right? Please tell me you didn't detonate a nuclear bomb under the sea."

"It wasn't a nuclear bomb, exactly. It was technology beyond my understanding. She used tachyons. I don't know. I trusted Mariela's aunt."

"So, you really detonated it?"

He nodded. "But instead of *bending* the fabric of space-time, it ripped a hole right through it."

"What?"

"I didn't realize it at first. I didn't know what I should expect. When I drove the sub back toward the surface, looking for the yacht, the boat wasn't there."

"Where was it?"

"At first, I thought the mission had been a success. I thought I had traveled back. Not wanting to start a war by possessing an alien sea craft in international waters, I anchored the sub and swam in scuba gear to the nearest land. That's when I realized the mission hadn't been a success."

She sighed with relief. So, maybe he wasn't delusional. Maybe Mariela's crazy aunt had convinced him to give time travel a try, and, as desperate as he was to save his wife, he had agreed, end of story.

"Instead of bending the fabric of space-time, we'd ruptured it, and I found myself on the first of many parallel worlds."

Denise's mouth fell open and she crossed her arms tightly in front of her. For many seconds, she stared at him, dumbfounded. All of this talk of parallel worlds was too much. "What led you to that conclusion?"

"I could tell by the technology that I hadn't gone back," he said. "But that didn't explain where the ship and Mariela's aunt had disappeared to. I returned to the marina, where we had docked the boat. No sign of her or the ship. I tried to call her but couldn't get a signal. I decided to go home, thinking maybe I'd been gone longer than I realized, that maybe I'd skipped *forward* in time."

She stared at him, studying his face for some sign that all of this was one big practical joke—that the love of her life wasn't insane. "What happened when you went home?"

"I met my doppleganger."

Denise covered her mouth. Markos couldn't be serious. "Markos, look at me. Are you playing a prank on me? Because I don't like this."

He took both of her hands and squeezed them. "I'm not playing a prank. I'm telling you what really happened. Please believe me. Trust me. I know it sounds crazy, but I'm telling you the truth."

Reluctantly, she nodded. "Okay. Okay, I'm listening."

"I hid from my doppleganger, not wanting to cause trouble. I watched him and was surprised to find him married—not to Mariela, but to her aunt. They had two little boys."

"Wasn't the aunt older?"

"No. She was younger. It was surreal. When I'd left her, she was twenty years older than me, and here she was, younger than me by six years. If I hadn't seen her with my doppleganger, I would have thought that maybe I *had* gone back in time—but his presence, along with the strange technology and other differences, mostly subtle, between our world and theirs convinced me that I was in an entirely different place altogether."

She covered her mouth and sat back in her chair, putting more distance between them. Trying to give him the benefit of the doubt, she asked, "What did you do?" Maybe he was telling the truth. Maybe he'd traveled to parallel worlds. She shivered. It seemed so unlikely, so impossible.

"I hid until they'd left the house. Then I broke in and found their computer. The system was unlike anything I'd seen, so it took me several hours to figure out how to use it, but, once I did, I was able to learn all about their world, including case studies of time travelers."

"Wait, are you saying the people on that world…"

"Had figured out how to travel back—not forward, only back. And their methods were still primitive. They had no ability to determine at what point in time their loop would intersect with the timeline. But their studies were over fifty years old, and, so far, each subject never went further back than the point at which they'd been born."

She scrutinized his face. Although he was excited, even agitated, he didn't seem to be crazy. But he had to be, right? He couldn't possibly have traveled to another world, a parallel world. Could he have? "So how did you get back to our world?"

"First, I volunteered to be a subject in their time-travel experiments. It would be six months from the time I applied to the time they would conduct the experiment, so I decided to return to my sub and try to get back to my own world, to check on Mariela. I had more nuclear devices on the craft, in case I needed to bend—or rip—space-time again.

"When I reached the trench, I could see a shimmering, bubbling region about twenty feet in diameter—nearly a perfect circle, but two-dimensional. I don't have the words to describe it, but I was convinced that it was the rupture I had created with my explosion and that it might be a portal back to my world. So, I drove the sub through it.

"I did as I had done before—I anchored the sub underwater to avoid a conflict in international waters. Then I swam in scuba gear up to the nearest island. It all looked familiar, but Mariela's aunt and our ship were not there waiting for me where I had left them.

"As before, I wondered if I'd been gone too long, and maybe she had returned home. But when I tried to get back to the marina, I quickly observed that the world was different. Again, the differences were subtle. For example, the telephone poles were shaped differently, and the traffic lights had different colors. The streets were paved with a different substance. They were spongier. The architecture was very different. The cars were similar, but different enough.

"I spent months going back and forth through the portal, trying to find either my world or the first I'd discovered. Through blind luck, I eventually made it back home, only to discover that Mariela had already passed. I'd been gone six months, according to her aunt, who was just as devastated as I was by the death of my wife."

Tears welled in his eyes. Denise wanted to comfort him, to tell him she would take him to a doctor and find him the right medication.

"I told Mariela's aunt about what I'd seen. We agreed that I should find a way back to that first parallel world, where I'd signed up to be a subject in the time-travel experiment. She went with me, having to see for herself, and she was the one who figured out how to navigate through the rupture to the literally hundreds of different worlds. We spent another six months traveling them together, picking up new technology and medical advancements, until we found the first world. I was almost turned down for the experiment, since I hadn't appeared for the trial six months prior and had set back their studies, but Mariela's aunt told them what had happened, and, after several more conversations during which she showed them her logs, maps, and calculations, they believed her.

"They sent me back in time, Denise."

Denise's head was spinning. She tried to hide her skepticism and her growing frustration and fear that this man, whom she thought was the love of her life, was delusional. He clearly believed what he was telling her. But maybe he was schizophrenic or had some other mental disorder. Maybe the grief over the loss of his wife had brought on whatever ailment he was clearly suffering from.

"Markos," she said. "I want to hear the rest of your story, I really do, but I don't feel well. Do you think you could take me home and tell me the rest on the way?"

He leaned across the table and cupped her face. The intimate gesture that had recently brought her chills of pleasure now gave her chills of dread.

"I'm sorry you don't feel well, but I can't take you home—not yet. I need to take you through the portal and show you the other worlds, so you can believe me, and so you will do what I need you to do."

Her mouth dropped open. He wanted her to do something? "What do you need me to do?"

He sucked in his lips and sighed. "Why don't you get some rest in your cabin, and we'll talk more tonight, at dinner? I'm going to fry up the fresh shrimp we bought in town. Okay?"

She studied his beautiful, tragic face and his sincere and stunning emerald eyes. He believed what he was saying, and that made him dangerous. If she went in the sub with him beneath the sea, what would happen when they *didn't* reach the world he was searching for—the world where he could save his dead wife? Denise took a deep breath and did the only thing she could. She smiled at Markos and said, "Okay."

Second Night at Sea

That afternoon, Denise locked herself in her cabin and wept.

She should have known her love affair with Markos had been too good to be true. She should have known that life couldn't be that glorious—not for a girl whose mother had died, whose father had shut down and become the child, and whose brother had abandoned her so he could survive. Denise should have known that Markos *hadn't* been the miracle that would save her life.

Markos was delusional. That was the only explanation that made sense. As much as she had enjoyed learning about gravitational waving, reverse magnetism, and the shimmering effect—as much as she had enjoyed pondering the notion of closed time-like curves—she couldn't accept that anyone could travel through time or discover parallel worlds. If so, more people would know about it. It would be in the news. There would be more evidence. And Markos wouldn't have had to take her to a secluded place to reveal his true motives.

She was on a ship in the middle of nowhere with a mentally unstable man.

Hoping to contact her father, or the police, or anyone that might rescue her, she reached across the bed to the nightstand for the device Markos had given her for Christmas, which was exactly like a smart phone. There was no signal. She searched her purse for her old phone, which she kept charged as a backup, but it had no signal, either.

What was she going to do?

She fell on the bed, curled up like a fetus, and tried to remain calm, but her body trembled, and the tears flowed, no matter how many times she said in her mind that everything was going to be okay.

Denise must have fallen asleep, because when she next awoke, the portal over her bed was a black circle. She checked the wristlet on her nightstand. It was already eight o'clock at night.

She brushed her teeth and hair, glaring at her reflection in the small mirror over the sink, willing all that Markos had said that afternoon to be nothing more than a nightmare.

"Please," she whispered after she'd rinsed and dried her mouth. "Let us go back to yesterday, before the craziness ruined everything."

A knock on her cabin door made her flinch.

"Denise?" Markos called from the corridor. "Are you okay?"

"I'll be right out," she replied.

Staring at her reflection, she willed everything back, back to where it was, even though she knew it to be impossible. She wanted to love Markos. She wanted to trust Markos. But, deep down, Denise was terrified of him.

She applied a cold wet cloth to her swollen eyes, trying to hold back the tears, but they came. She had another hard cry, and then, when she was too weak for any more tears, she slipped on her sandals and left her cabin.

She was startled to find Markos there, just outside her door, waiting for her. It had been at least ten minutes since he'd knocked, and he'd been standing there, waiting, all this time?

He took her in his arms. "You've been crying?"

She avoided his eyes as she nodded.

"Is it really so difficult for you to believe me?" he asked, tucking a strand of her hair behind her ear.

Denise shrugged and admitted, "I don't know what to think."

"Tell me." He kissed her nose. "What's going on in that incredible mind of yours."

As they walked, she said, "What would you think if our situations were reversed, Markos? I'm wondering if, like my father, something happened to you when your wife died, something that made you sick."

"Don't you think, as a medical doctor, I would know if I were sick?"

She shook her head. "Not necessarily, not if you're delusional."

He stepped back with clenched fists. "After all the trouble I went to, to track you down, to find out where and when you attended school, to convince your school to hire me, so I could teach you what you needed to know, to believe me. After all that, you're still not convinced? What? You think I'm insane?"

"What do you mean you tracked me down?" she asked, backing away.

"This was *your* idea! *You* are the one who convinced *me* to do this! And now you think I'm crazy?"

She furrowed her brows, totally perplexed. Had he lost it? Had he totally lost his mind?

"Calm down, Markos," she said softly. "Give me a chance to understand. I'm hungry. Can I have some dinner? Or did I miss it?"

He studied her face. She forced a smile, and when she looked hard into his emerald eyes, she felt a tug at her heart. If he *was* crazy, it wasn't his fault. She needed to be gentle and understanding, as she'd been with her father.

"Of course, you can have some dinner," he finally said. "It's all prepared. I've been waiting for you."

He took her hand and led her upstairs, where a cloudy night had fallen. Even the moon was shrouded in darkness. The dark night was also devoid of sounds—not even the gentle swoosh of waves against the anchored boat. Denise couldn't see beyond the ship's lights reflected in the water, only a few feet in all directions. It made her feel more afraid as she followed Markos into the kitchen, to the u-shaped bench around the square table by the picture window overlooking the ship's bow. She could see nothing beyond the deck. It was as if she and Markos and this ship were the only things in existence.

"I kept the fried shrimp warm in this paper sack," he said, as he served her. "But if it's not warm enough for you, let me know, and I can microwave it."

"I'm sure it's fine," she said.

"I made fresh coleslaw and fried potatoes to go with it," he said, as he continued to fill her plate. "And there's sun tea now, if you'd like it instead of Coke."

"Either one is fine," she said. "Thank you."

"Tartar sauce?" he asked.

"Yes, please."

She wasn't sure if she could eat, because her stomach was a ball of nerves, but once she tasted the delicious shrimp, her appetite returned, and she ate. When she had nearly finished her plate, she said, "It's delicious. You're a great cook."

"Like I said: I learned from the best."

"From Mariela's aunt?" she asked.

He winked—and it was goddamn sexy, in spite of how crazy he sounded: "From you."

"From *me*? I've cooked for you, what, two times?"

"Many more times than that."

So, he *was* delusional. Tears pricked her eyes, and she held her trembling hands beneath the table. "What are you talking about?"

"*You* are Mariela's aunt," he said.

Her mouth fell open, and she stared back at him for what must have been an entire minute.

"Are you saying that I'm from the future?" she finally asked.

"No. No, Denise. *You* aren't from the future. *I* am. And in twenty years, you will meet me as your niece's fiancé—not *this* me, but the me who was born a few years ago. Your *future you* is the one who convinced me to mess with the fabric of space-time. You were as hurt by Mariela's death as I was—probably because she was your world. You never married. You cared for your sick father, and you took all your joy from your brother's daughter."

"My brother, Girard?"

"That's why I tracked you down. When I went back in time, I ended up at the year of my birth. I returned to this world and waited, trying to figure out how to carry out our plan. That's when it hit me: I could convince your younger, past self to take Mariela to the doctor, long before she marries me. That's how we can save her, Denise. That's what I need you to do."

Denise squeezed her trembling hands together beneath the table, feeling both horrified and sorry for him at the same time.

At least he wasn't asking her to do something extraordinary; he just wanted her to take her niece to the doctor to have her checked for cancer.

"Oh, Markos." Denise covered her mouth. She'd had no idea how bad off he was—so much worse than her father had ever been. "Markos, did you ever consider the possibility that you created a fantasy, as a coping mechanism?"

"You still don't believe me? You still think I'm insane?" Now his face had paled, too.

"Not insane, just…"

"Listen to me. Didn't it occur to you that what I was teaching you in Introductory Physics was a different curriculum than what is usually taught in that course?"

"Yes. That's why I almost dropped it." Now she wished she had. "I just thought you were eccentric—in an interesting kind of way."

"I needed to lay down the foundation for *this* conversation!" He pounded his fist against the table on the word *this*. "But now it looks like that was all for nothing, because you don't believe me."

She stared back at him, unsure of what to say.

"And how did I know your Aunt Latisha was going to have a heart attack on Thanksgiving Day of 2017?" he challenged. "I'd almost forgotten, by the way. That's why I was late in getting there that day. I remembered at the last minute and had to make a special trip for the medicine I gave her. How could I have known if I wasn't from the future? I saved your aunt's life. Aren't you grateful?"

Denise shrugged. "Maybe she wasn't going to have a heart attack, Markos. Maybe this is all in your head."

He sat across from her, shaking his head as he stared across the room, for many minutes, saying nothing. Finally, he turned to her. "You're so smart." His face softened as he leaned across the table. "You really don't believe me? You can't even consider the possibility that I'm telling you the truth?"

"I'm considering it, Markos. I'm trying. Please be patient."

He put their plates in the sink and poured himself a coke and whiskey. "Want one?"

"No, thank you."

"I'm going to the upper deck. You're welcome to join me, or not. I need air."

Denise rinsed the dishes and loaded them into the mini dishwasher before joining Markos on the couch on the upper deck, where they had made love the night before. She desperately wished she could be that girl again—that girl who trusted and loved Markos with all her heart.

She hadn't been sitting beside him in the quiet, dark night for long, when he said, "Doesn't it seem strange to you that your niece is named Mariela, just like my wife? That you look so much like my wife?"

She didn't say what she was thinking—that maybe he had targeted her precisely because of her resemblance to his dead wife. She also couldn't say that she had no proof that he ever had a wife named Mariela. It could all be in his head.

But hadn't he told her his wife's name *before* she had told him Kassia and Girard's intention to name their daughter Mariela? He couldn't have managed that.

"When I came to dinner that Sunday after your niece was born," he said. "That was the hardest day of my life, even harder than the day I discovered that Mariela had passed away. To hold her as an infant—the woman I had loved, had married. That's when I finally realized how doomed your plan was from the beginning. Even if we could save Mariela, I could never be the one to be with her. My younger self would marry her. My younger self would spend his life with her, not me. I would be alone."

Denise's brain hurt. All this talk of future selves and younger selves—it was too much. "Markos…"

"But as you and I became closer, it hit me like a ton of bricks. Maybe you, not Mariela—maybe *you* were the love of my life."

"Markos…"

"Think about it, Denise. Don't say anything. Don't break my heart. Take some time to think about all I have told you. And tomorrow I'll prove to you that I'm speaking the truth."

Abruptly, Markos stood up and left the upper deck, leaving her alone in the dark night.

She sat on the couch where they had made love and thought over her situation, trying to think of ways to convince him to take her home. She sat for a very long time—at least an hour, thinking. She wondered if she could wait until he had fallen asleep, bring up the anchor, and then sail the ship to the nearest port. She went to the cockpit and studied the dashboard. She didn't know the first thing about how to operate the yacht. What if she got them killed?

Then she noticed the radio. Maybe she could call for help! She picked up the receiver, holding it to her lips, and squeezed the button on the side.

"Hello?" she said.

When nothing happened, she realized it must not be on. She searched the dash and found a dial, which she turned. Nothing happened, so she turned another dial. The radio came to life. She heard static and a man's voice breaking up.

"Hello?' she said again. "Can anyone hear me? I need help."

She worried she was making a mistake. If she could just convince Markos to take her home, she needn't worry about making him feel worse with a rescue mission, with his arrest, with whatever else would happen if she called for help.

"What's you're ten-twenty?" came the voice of the man.

"What's that mean?" Denise said.

"Where's your location? And what's the nature of your emergency?"

"The nature of my emergency is that…" She didn't know what to say, or if she was doing the right thing.

Suddenly Markos was beside her pulling the receiver from her hands. He turned off the radio. "What are you doing?"

"I'm frightened, Markos. I want to go home."

He grabbed her wrists, sending chills of fear across her skin. "Don't be frightened."

"You're hurting me."

He released her, looking mortified that his touch could hurt and frighten her. "Just let me show you proof. If, after tomorrow, you still want to go home, I'll take you. Okay?"

She searched his emerald eyes for signs of sanity. "Promise?"

He nodded. "After you see for yourself, after you see I'm telling the truth, you'll be fine." He put his arms around her waist. "We'll be fine."

She shuddered, and he felt it and pulled away, looking hurt.

"Markos, please understand how I feel. Your story is hard to imagine. Give me time, okay? Don't be hurt. Don't be angry with me."

She wrapped her arms around his neck and buried her face in his chest.

He held her close and whispered, "I'm not angry with you. I love you."

She wanted to say it back to him, but she couldn't. Her mind and heart were at odds with each other. She wanted to love him, but her mind echoed the words her father had told her: *Proceed with caution.*

That night, alone in her cabin, Denise couldn't sleep. The long nap she'd taken before dinner, coupled with her overwhelming fear that Markos was insane and unpredictable, had given her imagination free rein over her for hours. By four in the morning, she decided to leave her cabin and snoop around the ship.

She crept down the corridor to Markos's cabin door. When she turned the knob, she found it unlocked. Carefully, she pulled the door open. Markos lay in his bed, gently snoring. She could barely make out his features, as the only light in the room came from the soft glow of the square device on his bedside table. What she could see of him reminded her of how much she loved him: His sweet face, his irresistible body, and his soft and passionate lips invited her to hold him in her arms and comfort him. The fact that he was unstable didn't change the way she felt entirely. She would help him. She would convince him to see a professional. But first, she had to get them home safely before he did something from which there was no turning back.

She carefully closed the door and then took the steps upstairs, to the salon.

After turning on the lights, she searched every drawer and every cabinet in both the salon and the kitchen, hoping to find some clue as to his true intentions. She found nothing out of the ordinary—nothing that would give her insight into his condition.

She left the salon and climbed to the back deck, where the SEA-BOBS sat, and that's when an idea came to her: She would take the SEABOB to the nearest shore and get help. But the night sky was as dark as pitch, and the ocean was practically invisible to her. And who knew what was in the sea below the surface, waiting to eat her? No, she was safer on the ship with Markos than she would be out there.

She went to the cockpit and sat on one of the leather chairs, thinking about the radio. What would she tell someone if she made contact? Maybe she could lie and say there was a man overboard. That would get the Coast Guard to help them, wouldn't it? Was there a Coast Guard in this part of the world?

Tears streamed from her eyes as she wondered what in the hell she was going to do. Markos planned to take her to one of the other worlds in the morning. What would happen to a delusional man when faced with the stark truth? Or, worse, what if in the face of truth, his delusions continued, and he believed they were in parallel worlds, even when they weren't?

Was there any harm in going with him, just in case his bizarre story might be true?

C H A P T E R   T H I R T E E N

Third Day at Sea

When Denise woke up the next day, she stretched and looked around her room. The brightly lit portal to the beautiful sea over her bed drew her attention. She climbed to her knees and pressed her nose against the tempered glass. A school of clownfish a few yards away reminded her of Nemo from the animated motion picture *Finding Nemo*. For a moment, she delighted in watching them. Then her memories of what had transpired yesterday returned, and she groaned. It was too bad her father wasn't searching the sea for *her*.

After she showered and dressed in her bikini for the submarine ride, she stalled a little longer in her room, letting her imagination get the best of her. What if, in his madness, Markos accidentally got them killed?

She couldn't hide in her room all day. She went upstairs and found him in his swimming trunks in the kitchen, standing at the sink.

"Good morning, Sleeping Beauty," he said.

"Do they still know that fairytale in the future?" she asked.

"Does that mean you believe me?"

She shrugged. "Honestly. I still don't know what to think, Markos. I know I care for you, no matter what. If you're sick, I'll help you."

He took a deep breath and sighed. "This is all so ironic." He laughed, a bit too harshly for her comfort.

"How so?"

"This was *your* idea!" he said, allowing his frustration to get the better of him. "*Your* plan. And now your *past you* refuses to believe me."

She carefully crossed the room to stand before him at the sink and cupped his face in her hands. "It's not that I'm refusing to believe you. I'm trying. I really am."

He took another deep breath and slowly nodded. He covered one of her hands with his. "I know. I'm sorry." Then he asked, "Want some breakfast?"

Her stomach was in knots. "No, thanks."

"Then let's not wait another moment to make our journey, shall we?" he said. "I'm eager to prove to you that everything I've told you is true. Follow me."

She followed him below deck to the engineering room. Past the engine and other equipment was a chamber, and in it lay a small vessel that looked like a large green pickle with black rings on each end. It wasn't much larger than a twin-sized bed.

"That's the submarine?" she asked.

"It will be a tight fit," he said. "The cockpit, where the two of us will ride during the descent, is this sphere in the middle."

He pointed to a sphere with a diameter no bigger than the innertubes on which she'd floated down the Frio River each summer with her parents and brother when she was younger.

"This other sphere is a pressurized chamber where our scuba gear is. Everything else is mechanical—thrusters, weights, wiring, tubes, and such."

"Is it safe?" She had the ominous suspicion that getting into the contraption with him would mean certain death.

"There are always risks to every deep-sea expedition. But I promise you, it'll be worth it."

"What kinds of risks?"

"You and I have traveled in that sub dozens of times without a serious incident," he said. "Please trust me."

"What kinds of risks, Markos?"

"System failures, pressure leaks."

Her knees weakened. "Are you saying we could be killed?"

"We've taken dozens of trips together. I know you have no memory of them."

"How do I know they ever happened? How do I know those expeditions aren't part of your delusions?"

He sighed and closed his eyes, clenching his jaw. "Okay, let's think about this logically, then."

"Okay." She was curious how he could come up with any scenario that could be considered logical.

"If I'm delusional, it would have to be the most intricate and complicated delusion ever, considering the technology of this submarine. Come and have a look."

As technical as his descriptions of the sub's systems proved to be, she couldn't take the leap of faith he was asking of her.

He squeezed her arm. "While it's true that there is a small chance that the extreme pressure of being seven miles below the surface could crush us, there would be signs along the way, long before we were ever in that kind of danger, that would prompt me to abort the dive."

She shivered. "It still sounds scary."

"Now that you've imagined the worst-case scenario, consider the best," he said, taking her by the shoulders. "If all that I've said is true, you will have proof of it. Not only that, but you will bear witness to what no one else from your space-time has ever seen. You will travel with me to parallel worlds—to places where I retrieved the medicine for your father and aunt, where *we*—you and I—found a way back to save Mariela."

"But…"

"You can save Mariela. *We* can save her. Now, show me the adventurous spirit that I've come to know and love these past few years, Denise."

"Do I have a choice?" she challenged.

He sighed heavily again. "I suppose not."

As he helped her into her BCD, he said, "We won't be wearing any of our gear except for these vests. There's not enough room in the cockpit. But once I anchor us, we'll enter the pressure chamber and strap on our gear before swimming to the surface of the other world."

Denise's teeth chattered uncontrollably. She wished she could talk to her father. Tears pricked her eyes as she imagined her father's face and his kind voice. She hoped she would see him again.

"Don't be frightened," Markos said gently.

She gave him a pleading look. "I don't want to die."

"You won't," he said. "I promise."

The word of a mad man meant nothing to her.

He helped her into the compact sphere and closed and bolted the hatch. They sat facing one another with their knees bent. His legs were open, and his feet were planted on either side of her hips, his knees cradling her. Her legs were together, her feet tucked beneath his seat, her knees pressed between his chest and hers.

"It's a good thing I'm not claustrophobic," she muttered.

"I already knew that about you," he said in a way that was probably meant to be reassuring.

As she watched him tighten the bolt to the hatch overhead, she couldn't escape the feeling that she had just entered her coffin and was about to be buried alive beneath the sea.

"Strap yourself in," he said. "Once we descend, the vehicle will turn vertical."

The sub came to life as Markos flipped different switches. It began to hum and to vibrate. Lights came on both inside the cockpit and outside. She could see the outer chamber through two glass portals the size of tea saucers located on either side of her.

He embraced her knees. "Here we go."

He pushed a button, causing the hatch in the hull of the yacht to slide open. Water poured into the chamber and surrounded the sub.

Tears fell down Denise's cheeks. Her throat tightened with fear. She could barely breathe.

"This is when you usually say. 'Adventure awaits,'" he said.

She gave him a half smile and choked out, "Adventure awaits."

He wiped her tears with his thumb. "I won't let anything happen to you."

Once the chamber was full of water, Markos launched the sub from the hull of the yacht. They shot out with great speed into the sea and then immediately began to sink toward the ocean floor. She was above him, held in place by the harness strapping her in and the pressure of her knees against Markos's chest as gravity pulled her toward him.

"What's happening?" she asked.

"We're making our descent," he said, looking up at her. "I'm glad you're with me. You can't imagine how alone one feels in a small vessel in the deepest part of the ocean."

Denise shuddered. "How long will it take us to get there?"

"A few hours, but not to worry. See this?" He held up the cube-shaped device she'd seen him with so many times. "I have some of my favorite movies stored on this. Anything particular you'd like to watch?"

She glanced outside the portal to her left.

"You'd probably rather look at the wildlife," he said, "since, technically, this is your first descent."

The lights on the outside of the sub made it possible for her to see glimpses of sea creatures that came within ten or so yards of the sub. She saw jelly fish, schools of multi-colored fish, a sand shark, and many other single fish that swam up to the portal, curious about the vehicle. Markos told her what he knew of the wildlife. After a half hour, she began to feel better.

"Uh-oh," Markos said, looking at the controls over her head.

"What's wrong?"

"My depth gauge is no longer working."

"What does that mean?"

"It means I can't tell how deep we are."

"Is that a problem?"

"Not as long as we don't hit bottom at our current speed." He flipped another switch. "No, no no."

Her stomach dropped, and she could barely breathe. "Markos, you're scaring me."

"Something's wrong with my thrusters. They aren't working."

"If your thrusters don't work, how can you stop us from hitting the ocean floor?"

"I can't." He continued to flip switches above her head. She wondered if he even knew what the hell he was doing. Maybe the switches did nothing. He'd bought them a very expensive coffin to bury them in.

Denise caught her reflection in one of the portals. Her eyes were wide, her mouth open, and, even though she usually breathed through her nose, she was panting through her mouth, her nostrils flaring.

"What will happen if we crash?' she asked. And when he didn't answer right away, she asked again.

"Calm down, Denise." He pushed another button, and she felt the vehicle slow down. "Focus on your breathing, nice and slow, in and out."

"What are you doing?' she asked. "Are the thrusters working?"

"I'm dropping weight," he said. "It's going to be okay."

She clutched her chest, which was tight with fear. "How will we get back to the yacht without thrusters?"

"This has happened before," he said, as he opened a panel above her head and took a screwdriver to it. "I know how to repair the problem. Calm down."

"And if you can't? Just tell me what will happen, Markos, even if you believe it's unlikely."

"What good would that do?" he said with a tinge of reproach.

"I want to prepare myself. It's how I am."

"That's *not* how you are. You're *the glass is half full*, the *nothing's impossible*, the *go for it* kind of person. I know you better than you know yourself."

"That's not me. That's someone else."

"I'm inflating the tubes," he said. "Even without thrusters, they'll get us to the surface."

She heard a loud whoosh just before the sub jerked to a stop and then began climbing upward. She closed her eyes and focused on her breathing as she convinced herself that everything was going to be alright.

As Markos worked on the control panel above her head, he talked to her, but she was too busy praying. She was numb and unable to process anything he said. When the sub reached the surface, Markos had to snap her out of her prayers to get her to notice.

"We made it back?" she asked, incredulous. She'd been convinced they were going to die.

"Listen to me," he said. "I can usually drive the sub right back into the hull of my yacht, but without thrusters, I can't do that."

"Can't we just climb out and swim to safety?" she asked.

He nodded. "First we'll put on our scuba gear. Then we'll exit the sub and get our bearings. The compass still works, so I think we're about a half-mile east of the yacht. We'll have to paddle to the ship, however far it is. Understand? I'm not abandoning the sub, even for a minute."

He opened a second hatch to another spherical compartment behind her. After they climbed through the narrow opening, Markos bolted down the hatch to the cockpit and then helped her into her gear before he strapped on his own.

"When I open this door, this part of the sub will fill with water. Once it's completely full, the pressure will stabilize, and we can swim to the surface and climb on top of the sub."

"Won't it sink once the water gets in?"

He shook his head. "That's why this sphere is even smaller than the cockpit."

"Okay."

"Ready?"

She pressed her mask against her face and sealed her mouth around her regulator. Then she nodded. Markos opened the tiny hatch by pulling it inward, and the water flooded in. It was cold as it crept against her skin, rising to her throat, to her nose, to her eyes.

Markos helped her swim out of the sub. Then he held her hand and placed it on one of the black rings. He put one of her feet on a ring below. The black rings were handles, or steps, like a ladder. She climbed her way up to the top of the sub. Once she had straddled the sub, with Markos in front of her, she pulled her regulator from her lips, gasped for air, and scoured the horizon for the ship. It was nowhere in sight.

Markos handed her a paddle. "It's just west of us. I'm sure of it."

She watched his back and followed his lead as best as she could with the paddle. The sub seemed to barely move with each stroke. At least the water was relatively smooth, the sky clear and blue, and the sun blazing down from high noon. In no time, she was dry and no longer cold, and she was very, very happy to be alive.

C H A P T E R F O U R T E E N

Third Night at Sea

Once they were safely back on board the yacht and climbing out of their scuba gear in the engineering room, Denise asked Markos if he would take her home.

"What?" he seemed surprised. "Are you kidding? No. I'm going to repair the sub. We'll try again in the morning."

The cold, sharp shivers of fear tingled down her spine. "But you promised."

"I said I'd take you home after I show you the truth," he said.

She took a few strides to him, his beautiful body glistening with water. "Please don't put me through that again, Markos. I was so frightened. I thought we were going to die."

He wrapped his arms around her waist. "You were never in any danger. I promise I won't let anything happen to you. Please. If you ever loved me, give me this chance to prove to you that I'm telling you the truth."

This situation seemed so hopeless. She was doomed, utterly doomed. With weakened knees, she fell against him, her tears mixing with the water dripping on their skin.

"Don't cry," he said softly. "This will all be over soon, and then we can go back to how things were."

She couldn't imagine that such a thing was possible. Even if they survived the next launch, even if she managed to get back home to safety, and even if she convinced him to get medical attention, she wasn't sure that she could ever feel the way she had felt about him two days ago, before he'd revealed his plan.

"Why don't you go and get cleaned up, and then make yourself a sandwich while I get to work on the sub?" he suggested.

She nodded and returned to her cabin, while every muscle in her body trembled. As she stripped and got into the shower, allowing the warm water to wash over her, she imagined the countless times she had taken her father's gun and had held it to her temple. She'd wanted to end her life so desperately and hadn't been brave enough to do it. Now, here she was, most likely about to die, and the only thing she felt was the overwhelming desire to live.

A few hours later, she went above deck to the kitchen, feeling hungry for the first time that day. There was no sign of Markos, so she imagined he must be down in the engineering room, working on the sub. After making herself a sandwich, she took her plate to the upper deck and sat on the couch facing the west, where the sun was waiting to make its descent.

The beauty of the clear blue sky and the sparkling green sea stretching for miles mocked her. The seagulls flying past with their shrill calls taunted her. Everything around her seemed to be saying, "Well, you wanted to die, didn't you?"

She couldn't eat the second half of her sandwich as she thought about having to endure another launch in the sub the next day. It had been the most terrifying thing she'd ever experienced—even more frightening than the day her mother had died. That day had been sad, but the accident had happened so quickly, that Denise hadn't had time to be afraid. It had been a sorrowful day, a miserable day, a day for crying uncontrollably at all hours; however, it hadn't been a day of terror.

As she returned to the kitchen, she told herself that she had to think of a way to avoid the launch. Could she feign illness? No, he'd take her anyway. Should she try the radio? If so, what would she say? And who would come? And what if Markos convinced whoever might come that the radio call was a false alarm? Should she take a chance on the SEABOB?

The previous night, she'd been convinced that she was safer on the yacht than out in the open sea with the SEABOB, but now that she'd survived Markos's attempt to descend to the depths of the Mariana Trench in a malfunctioning sub, she questioned her decision. She scraped the second half of her sandwich into the trash and rinsed her plate in the sink before drying it and returning it to the cabinet, all the while thinking of this new idea.

Her scuba gear was still in the engineering room, where Markos was working on the sub. There was no way she could risk taking the SEABOB without scuba gear. But could she get her gear without being seen by Markos? She crept down the stairs below deck.

When she opened the door, she saw Markos. He was bent over the sub with his upper body hidden inside the cockpit. Slowly, she reached down and collected her gear from the floor, where she'd removed it. Then she made her way out of the room, closing the door behind her.

Her heart was beating fast when she climbed to the back deck, where the SEABOBs were stored. Without taking the time to change into her swimsuit, she quickly strapped on her BCD, tank, mask, and flippers, wearing her shorts and tank top. Then, just as Markos had done, she pushed the SEABOB off the back of the boat, where it floated in the water. She slipped in beside it, grabbed it by the handles, and turned it on.

What would Markos do when he discovered what she'd done? She couldn't imagine how frustrated he would be—and how hurt. But he'd promised her he'd take her home after their launch, and he hadn't kept his word. She had every right to distrust him, every right to do what she could to save herself. Full of guilt and fear, she sped away from the yacht toward the west, toward the sun, hoping her SEABOB could outswim the sharks.

As she fled across the open sea, she glanced back at the yacht every few minutes, expecting to see Markos coming after her; but, instead, the ship became more and more distant until it disappeared from her view altogether. She could see nothing now but ocean in all directions.

Alone on the large expanse of sea without another thing in sight, she tried not to think about the fact that the ocean below her teemed with creatures, some of which were predators wanting to eat her. She kept her sights on the sun. At least she knew she wasn't going in circles. With the sun as her guide, she could make it to Guam. It had taken the yacht only a few hours to travel from Apra Harbor to its current location. Denise wasn't sure how the speed of the SEABOB compared to that of the yacht, but she imagined it would take the SEABOB at least twice as long. The sun would set in a few hours, but she didn't have to get all the way to Apra Harbor. She just needed to be seen by one of the other ships in the area—and there had been many. One of them was bound to see her.

She drove on. As she would breach each new set of waves in the limited view before her, she would expect to find something that could save her—whether land or vessel. This hope propelled her for over half an hour, but the appearance of clouds in the sky—not white puffs of cotton, but gray and swollen—challenged her hope with a new threat. She felt it in the water, too. It was getting colder, more agitated. What had been waves with crests no more than one or two feet grew to three and four feet in height. The SEABOB struggled, as the waves came from more than one direction, tossing her this way and that, and the sun—her one beacon of hope was now hidden.

Tears of frustration and of fear enveloped her eyes as she gripped the handles of the SEABOB. She could not die like this, out in the middle of nowhere. She had to be strong. Maybe the sea would be easier to manage below the surface. She'd lost sight of the sun, so the benefit of being on the surface had been lost. She fitted her mask to her face, sealed her lips around her regulator, and pressed the submerge button on the dashboard of the SEABOB.

She was shocked to see the ocean floor about twenty feet from the surface, covered in colorful anemone and puffer fish. The shallower water was a good sign, wasn't it? Didn't it mean she was getting closer to land?

The change in weather was evident below the surface as much as it had been above. A strong current pressed against the SEABOB, and she was no longer confident that she was swimming toward the west.

She followed the ocean floor, searching for a slope, hoping it could lead her, like the sun had, toward her salvation; but it was flat. Then she remembered that there was a compass on her BCD, she reached for it and found the needle pointing southwest. She cursed in her head as she maneuvered the SEABOB until the needle was pointing west, and then, full of both frustration and hope, sped onward with one eye on the compass and the other on the ocean floor below.

She passed a bed full of large shrimp, after which, she barely missed dodging a huge school of silver fish. Just beyond the school was something that made her heart stop beating in her chest—at least that's how it felt as mortal fear coursed through her veins. It was a large shark, almost as large as she was, and it was swimming her way.

She'd always been told that you shouldn't flee from a shark, and yet her instinct was to do that very thing. She fought her instinct and idled on the SEABOB, keeping her eye on the beast. The shark seemed unaware of her. She prayed he would move on as she hung there, limp, quivering, nearly hysterical with fear.

Then the shark noticed her. Denise gasped and stopped breathing. Except for her trembling, she was still, and it was almost as if she had floated outside of her body and was watching the shark looking at her. The beast swam toward her—not quickly, but as if he were curious about her. He was so close to her that she could see one of his eyes. She wanted to kick and scream and flee, but, instead, she closed her eyes and prayed. She kept her eyes closed for nearly a minute before she opened them again. The shark was gone.

Denise headed for the surface, deciding it was better not to know what was swimming in the depths below her. When she emerged, she was pelted by rain and she could see nothing beyond a few feet in front of her. Using her compass, she headed west, though it was slow going over the swells.

Without the sun, it was impossible to figure out what time it was or how much time she had before darkness fell. She wished she had stayed on the damn ship. Over and over, she asked herself, "Why didn't you stay on the damn ship?"

From out of nowhere, and quite suddenly, a gigantic wave lifted her up. From her perspective, it felt like a tsunami. She gripped the SEA-BOB as she was flung across the top of the crest, where, in the distance, she saw the enormous hull of a cargo ship.

Through a dry and tight throat, Denise shouted, "Hey! Hey, over here!"

The rain beat down on her, almost as if the earth itself did not want her to be saved.

She waved an arm as high as she could reach, and nearly slipped from the SEABOB.

"Hey!" she shouted again. "Please! Over here!"

The ship moved past her in less than a minute. She turned her SEA-BOB in its direction, trying to follow, but she was thrown off course by its incredible wake.

"Wait!" she cried again and again as her tears streamed down her soaking face and as she fought against the water, tossing her aside like a useless thing.

Her efforts were futile. The ship soon disappeared from her view, and she was, once again, alone.

Or *not* alone, she reminded herself as she thought of the shark and other creatures below her.

She plodded on toward the west, doubtful that she was making any progress other than maintaining herself on the surface of the huge peaks and valleys that came with every swell. Desperate, she oscillated between hope and despair, between muttering, "Why didn't you stay on the damn ship?" and "Please, God, get me out of this."

When the rain finally stopped, she was grateful. "Thank you, God. Even if I die, thank you for taking away the rain."

She plodded on, going nowhere, it seemed.

Although she felt like a tiny speck on the gigantic, churning sea, Denise had believed she would find land before nightfall; so, when night engulfed her in its dark and lonely blanket, she was honestly surprised. Her body convulsed with wracking sobs as she thought, maybe Markos had been right: she was a *glass is half full* kind of person, and that was why she had ever considered taking the SEABOB and fleeing. She had truly believed she would make it, that her story wouldn't end with her death at sea. As terrified as she had been, a part of her had never lost hope.

But now, faced with the thick veil of pitch and unable to see beyond the soft glowing light on her SEABOB dashboard, there was no more hope. As if the earth wanted to mock her still, the SEABOB engine sputtered feebly for a few seconds and stopped.

She laid her cheek against the dashboard and wept, thinking it hadn't been such a bad life. She'd loved her family and she'd loved Markos, and love was the point, wasn't it? And soon, maybe she would see her mom.

The thought of reuniting with her mother triggered another wave of convulsing sobs. But now, she filled again with hope—not a hope of survival, but a hope of seeing her mother, whom she had missed with the aching, gut-wrenching, painful longing that no one who hadn't lost a parent could comprehend.

"Mom?" she whispered against the dash of the SEABOB. "Mom, are you there?"

Denise must have fallen asleep on the lonely sea, because she was startled awake when her leg scraped against something rough. She flinched from the contact and assessed her surroundings. The first thing she noticed was that she no longer had the SEABOB. Her BCD was the only thing holding her afloat. The next thing she noticed was that the sun had returned for early dawn. And the third thing she noticed was a huge rock jetting from the sea.

Her feet struck bottom and she climbed through the water toward the rock.

The rock was about ten feet tall and eight feet in diameter. It was covered near the base in algae, and a few small crabs. She climbed as far up as she could reach—about two feet from the summit—and gazed as far out as she could see.

She saw no signs of other land, but she did see a ship, and it was coming toward her. As the ship neared, hope bloomed in her chest with a subtle pang of despair as she realized she would not be meeting her mom.

"Wait for me, Mom," she whispered. "I'm not coming yet."

CHAPTER FIFTEEN

First Sign

Denise clung to the rock jetting out of the sea as she watched the ship approach. The hope that had filled her heart diminished when she began to fear that the vessel coming toward her belonged to Markos. It was the same color, same size, same shape. When the bow became visible and she saw its name painted in black, tears of frustration pricked her eyes.

It was *The Mariela*.

The yacht stopped twenty yards away, and, not long after, she spotted Markos on his SEABOB heading for her.

"My, God, Denise! Are you okay?" he said as he approached. "I was worried sick. Thank God you're alive."

She said nothing as he helped her trembling body from the rock to the SEABOB, putting her between him and the machine.

"Let's get you back to safety," he said, and it took every bit of self-control for her not to laugh at the irony of his words.

Once Markos had helped her aboard, Denise's first words were, "I'm thirsty."

He led her to the kitchen for fresh water. As she drank it down, he asked her what had happened.

On the ride from the rock, she'd considered telling him that she had intended only to explore near the ship on the SEABOB, to pass the time. She was going to say that she'd been swept away and lost at sea by accident; but, when he moved her hair from her face and looked at her with his supremely beautiful emerald eyes, she found herself unable to tell him anything but the truth. In spite of his delusions, she loved him. It wasn't his fault that he was sick. She doubted she could ever feel the same way about him as she had felt before he'd begun his story, but that didn't mean she didn't love him.

Once he'd heard her story—she'd feared for her life, and she couldn't bear to descend in the sub to the bottom of the sea another time—he didn't get angry. He sighed, closed his eyes, and sucked in his lips. Then he nodded as he looked at her with tears in his eyes.

"I understand," he finally said. "Why don't you get cleaned up. Get some rest. I'll make you something to eat, when you're ready."

"Did you fix the sub?" she asked with quivering lips.

"Yes."

Her knees trembled.

"But don't worry," he said. "I won't make you go again."

Her mouth fell open, and her eyes widened with surprise. "Really? You won't?"

He shook his head. "I'm sorry, Denise. I had no idea how terrified you were. Honestly."

She sighed heavily, as relief washed over her. She felt as though she might collapse right there on the deck.

"Do you need my help getting down to your cabin?" he asked.

She probably did, but she said she didn't as she turned away and left.

An hour later, after she'd showered, dressed, and lain on her bed, she left her cabin in search of Markos. Above deck, she spotted land in the distance, and there were other ships nearby. He was taking her back to Apra Harbor in Guam. Soon she would be home, with her father. She would see her loved ones again. She would return to her ordinary life. Once again, relief swept over her, and she was so very glad to be alive.

She found Markos in the cockpit. He gave her a half smile and then averted his eyes, back to the sea.

"Do you mind if I sit here?" she asked.

"Of course not," he replied.

She sat on the chair adjacent to his and gazed at the land before them.

After a few moments of silence, she said, "Thank you."

"You have no reason to thank me," he said without looking at her. "In carrying out our—my—plan, I had no idea of the toll it would take on you. For that, I'm truly sorry, Denise."

She had no words.

Finally, he looked at her, and she saw that tears were streaming down his cheeks. She wanted to hold him and tell him that it was going to be okay; but the truth was, she didn't know if it would be for him. He might be too far gone for medical help.

"I made you some sandwiches and cut up the rest of the fruit," he said as he wiped the tears from his cheeks. "It needs to be eaten."

"Thanks. I'll go down in a minute."

He nodded and looked back out to see, toward Guam.

After they sat there for many more minutes with nothing but the sounds of the wind and the waves and the gentle hum of the ship's engine, Denise stood up and said, "I guess I'll go eat now."

"Denise?"

She turned to face him. "Yes?"

"I meant what I said about being sorry, about never intending to frighten you. I hope you believe me. I hope you know how much I still love you."

Unable to resist his emerald eyes and his other beautiful features—dark hair, strong jaw, brooding brows—she crossed the deck and kissed his forehead. She allowed her lips to linger on his skin for several seconds before she pulled away and said, "I know, Markos. I still love you, too."

He gave her wry grin. "Even though you think I'm crazy?"

What could she say? "You helped my father. Maybe I can help you."

Now he laughed ruefully, and it made her sad. When he saw her frown, he stood up and cupped her cheeks.

"Just promise me one thing, sweet, sweet Denise."

She looked up at his sad, lovely face.

"Make sure Mariela sees a specialist before her seventeenth birthday."

Denise averted her eyes, trying not to roll them and suppressing the heavy sigh in her heart.

"What harm could that do?" he added. "Even if I'm crazy, and this is all my delusion, it will hurt no one for you to make me that promise."

He was right. "I promise, Markos. I will take Mariela to the doctor."

"By her seventeenth birthday," he repeated.

"Yes. I will. Okay?"

He released her as more tears filled his eyes. "Thank you."

When Denise stepped off *The Mariela* and onto the dock in Apra Harbor, joy and relief filled her heart. She felt as though she had descended into the bowels of the earth, into the Underworld itself, and had returned reborn.

She slept for most of their flights, unable to bear Markos's sadness. But during the flight from LA to San Antonio, she was wide awake. After sitting quietly beside her for many minutes, Markos unexpectedly took her hand and said, "I want to tell you something, Denise."

She studied his face. It had never looked so sad. "I'm listening."

"I know you think I'm crazy," he said. "And I wish you were right, because then all I'd have to do would be to get professional help and then we could be together."

"Markos…"

"Unfortunately, I'm not. Everything I've told you is the truth, but…" He took a deep breath. "But I understand why you can't believe me."

"Thank you."

"And I also understand why we can't be together," he added.

Her eyes filled with tears.

"But I want to tell you about your future," he said. "Not everything—that wouldn't be right. But I want to tell you enough details so that one day you will know that everything I said was true."

He was beautifully tragic—his sincerity, his intensity, his passion. She wished she could believe him. She wished she could love him like she had before. "I'm listening."

"You're going to graduate from Trinity University with a bachelor's degree in physics in 2021."

"I hope so," she said with a smile.

"Then, you're going to get a scholarship to attend graduate school at Harvard because of a paper you publish proving that objects are capable of surpassing the speed of light."

She bit her lip, thinking, *If only*.

"You'll earn your Ph.D. in physics over the next six years, and the topic of your dissertation will be on special applications of Godel's closed time-like curves."

"How do I know that your predictions won't be causing my choices?" she pointed out.

He smiled. "Of course, *you* would think of that."

She returned his smile with a shrug.

"You could be right that what I'm telling you will change the course of your life as I knew it," he said. "I already changed it when I came back and told you my story—even before that, when I saved you from Hex. I couldn't stand by, knowing what had happened to you."

"What? You mean that night at the club?"

He gave her a sideways glance. "I shouldn't have told you that."

"You're saying the Denise you believe you know from the future was…"

"Never mind," he said. "But the Denise I knew never married, and, until recently, I thought it was because of your on-again, off-again relationship with that boy, Brian."

"Brian Jameson? Your student?"

"Avoid him, Denise. He may have had real feelings for you, but something was broken in him. He never gave you what you needed. *You* told me that."

She sat in stunned silence. How could he know anything about Brian?

"But after coming back here and getting to know *this* you, I realized it was your devotion to your sick father that kept you from finding someone."

"My father isn't sick anymore," she said.

"Another example of how I've changed your future," he said. "So maybe now, you *will* find someone. Maybe you *will* get married."

He spoke with such sadness and regret that it pained her to listen to him. "Markos…"

"I suppose the real proof won't come for you until you meet Mariela's fiancé in the year 2036."

"That's nineteen years from now," she said.

"Unless the future dramatically changes because of my trip back, Mariela will marry Markos Nadir in 2037 in San Antonio at the First Baptist Church on Lockwood Street on Saturday, December 29th, at two in the afternoon, with a cake and punch reception following."

Denise couldn't take any more of his madness. She wanted him to stop. "Okay, Markos. But I don't know which outcome would be more tragic—that you're right and I miss out on the love of my life, or that you're wrong and a terrible illness got the best of a man I loved."

He furrowed his brows. "You're right, as usual, oh, Smart One."

Although his voice was half rueful, it was also playful, and she laughed.

Then he said, "I need a drink."

When Markos drove her home from the airport, he declined her invitation to come inside. The late afternoon sun was beginning its descent when he pulled up to the curb, helped her with her luggage, and walked her to the front door.

They stood facing one another beneath the portico. He smoothed her hair from her face and cupped her cheeks as his beautiful emerald eyes gazed down at her.

"I still believe you're the love of my life, Denise," he said in a broken voice. "I'm going to miss you."

An aching need to hold him compelled her arms around his neck. "Oh, Markos. Please at least consider the possibility…"

"It's no use," he said. "But someday, you'll come to realize it. And when you do, I hope you'll think of me fondly and not as some crazy man who once frightened you."

She closed her eyes as he pressed his sweet lips to hers.

"Goodbye," he said before he turned and abruptly walked away.

She watched him hasten down the sidewalk to climb, quickly, into his car, as if he couldn't bear to be around her for another moment. He didn't look at her again before he drove off. Tears dropped down her cheeks, and a pang in her heart urged her to consider the possibility that maybe, just maybe, he *had* been telling her the truth.

Her father was on the living-room sofa reading beneath the light of a floor lamp when she walked in the door. The smile that spread across his face when his eyes met hers filled her heart with joy. She'd thought she'd never see him again. The experience on the ship had made her come to terms with the hate and resentment she'd felt toward him, the blame she placed on him for her mother's death; but, it had also made her long to see him. Despite her feelings about what happened six years ago, she loved her father. She ran to embrace him.

"Hello, Baby," he said. "I missed you."

Tears fell down her cheeks, and her throat tightened. She couldn't speak.

"Denise?" he asked, rubbing her back as she clung to him, unable to pull away. "What's the matter, Baby? Did something happen?"

She sat beside him on the couch, unsure of whether to tell him the truth. On the one hand, it would bring her comfort to share her story with him and to have him tell her everything was going to be just fine. On the other hand, she didn't want to frighten him and to make him fear that Markos would bring harm to her and to their family. She truly believed Markos was no longer a threat to them, and she didn't want her father to worry needlessly.

Ultimately, she said, "I'm just so happy to be home, Daddy."

Over the weekend, Denise got some much-needed rest, but there were still things she needed to do. She had a paper to edit before Monday. And because her father had grown accustomed to *her* doing the grocery-shopping, they were out of food, so she went. And since he'd never learned to cook and had eaten take-out and frozen dinners in her absence, she prepared some healthy meals.

She wore her sapphire pendant, and every time she saw her reflection in the mirror, she clutched it and thought of Markos.

For their traditional family gathering on Sunday, she baked a lemon cream cake, in honor of the good memories she had of Markos. It was her mission to focus on the good and to forget what had happened on his yacht.

While her brother and his family visited on Sunday afternoon, Denise held her niece, wondering if there was any possibility that she would grow up to marry Markos Nadir. Worried that she was somehow catching the sickness that controlled Markos, Denise dismissed the idea and focused on being in the present with this sweet, precious baby, whom she loved with all her heart.

On Monday, Denise was walking from her literature class to her political science class when someone caught her elbow. She expected—and hoped—to see Markos, but when she turned, she found Brian.

"Did you hear about Professor Nadir?" he asked her.

"Oh, no." She covered her mouth, expecting the worst. "What?"

"He left his position. Just walked out. The school is scrambling to replace him."

Denise shouldn't have been surprised, but she was. "Do you know why?"

"The administrator in the Physics Department told me he left for personal reasons," Brian said. "Any ideas what those reasons could be?"

Denise frowned. "The last time I spoke to him, he seemed ill. Maybe he left because of health problems."

Brian shrugged. "I thought maybe he left because of you."

She glared at him. "What? No. I told you. We aren't a thing."

Brian squeezed her shoulder. "Relax. Don't get so mad. I'm sorry."

"It's okay. I'm sorry, too."

Brian took a step back and looked her over. "Are you feeling okay?"

"I'm fine. I need to get to class."

She started to walk away when he grabbed her elbow again. "Wait. Any chance you'd have dinner with me again? As friends?"

Denise studied his face, recalling Markos's warning: *Brian had feelings for you but he was broken and could never give you what you needed.*

Finally, she said, "I don't think that's a good idea, but thanks, anyway."

CHAPTER SIXTEEN

Second Sign

Denise threw herself into her studies and into her job doing hair but she couldn't stop thinking of Markos and of the unlikely possibility that he had told her the truth.

Unlikely but not impossible, she thought.

One Friday night in late April, she sat on her bed with her laptop, checking her grades online, when she decided to Google Markos again. The search brought up the same results as it had the last time. Then, a new idea occurred to her, and, with trembling fingers, she typed into the search bar: *birth records New York*.

Visits to various websites thwarted her at every turn. There didn't seem to be a way for her to obtain the birth certificate of someone unrelated to her. But then she stumbled upon a genealogy website.

The website only required a first and last name, a birth year, and a birth location.

Markos claimed to have come back to the year of his birth, and he'd taught at Harvard for two years before moving to Trinity.

Clutching her sapphire pendant, she typed: *Markos Nadir, 2015, New York, New York*. Holding her breath, she hit *enter*.

The search brought up zero results.

Of course, it had, she thought. What had she expected? Had she really believed it was possible that a younger version of Markos existed? She shook her head, mentally berating herself. She was pathetic, desperate, and foolish.

She kept the laptop open to the site, wanting to try other years. Maybe he'd been born in 2014, or 2016. But then she snapped the laptop closed, chiding herself for entertaining such fantastical delusions.

Needing a distraction, she picked up her phone and texted Brian.

What are you doing? she wrote.

When he didn't answer, she again told herself that she was pathetic. She slammed her phone down on her bed and clenched her jaw, trying not to cry. Desperate, pathetic, and foolish. Maybe she needed professional help, too.

She thought of her father's gun still tucked in the drawer of her bedside table.

No. You will not go there, she told herself as her hand reached for the drawer.

Her phone buzzed, drawing her from her reverie. It was Brian.

On my way to Whataburger. Wanna join me?

Denise bit her lip wondering what the hell she was doing texting Brian; but, of their own accord, her fingers typed: *Which one?*

Rigsby, came his reply.

She quickly wrote: *On my way…*

Denise wasn't hungry, so she drank a Coke while Brian ate a burger and fries, and it was nice to talk about high school, about mutual friends, about college, about aspirations—even about math. After he'd finished eating, he asked if she wanted to check out his new apartment.

"You moved out?"

"About time," he said with a laugh.

"Where is it?"

"Just up the road. Nothing fancy."

They decided to leave her car and come back for it later.

As she climbed into the passenger side of his truck, he said, "I just need to pick up some whisky on the way. You okay with that?"

She shrugged. "How long will that take?"

"A few minutes."

She waited in his truck while he ran inside the liquor store. He'd been right: he returned within five minutes.

Like her, he'd come from a family that had always struggled with money. And, like her, he'd won a full ride to Trinity. It was the only way either of them would have been able to attend such a prestigious school. While the scholarship paid for tuition and books, it didn't cover room and board, so she wasn't surprised when he pulled up to a rundown apartment complex that reminded her of the government housing projects.

"Like I said, nothing fancy," he repeated.

"It's your own place," she said with a smile. "That's something to be proud of."

"I guess."

She followed him up the concrete steps to his second-floor unit, where he opened the door and turned on a lamp.

The floor lamp and one old couch were the only furnishings in the small living area. He had no table or chairs, but there was a peninsula in the tiny kitchen with a couple of cheap metal barstools.

When he looked for her reaction, she said, "Cozy."

He laughed. "That's a nice way to put it."

He showed her his bedroom and bath and then asked, "Wanna drink?"

"Why not?" she said.

"Want it with Sprite?" he asked. "I don't have any Coke."

"Sprite works."

"Have a seat." He gestured toward the couch. "Take a load off."

Her bottom nearly sank to the floor when she sat on the couch, but she stifled a laugh as he joined her with their drinks.

"I don't have a television yet. Saving up for one."

"I don't watch it much, anyway," she said. "Only when I'm braiding hair."

"I'm glad you texted me tonight," he said. "I was bored out of my mind. I thought I'd love having my own place, but, to tell you the truth, it's been lonely."

"Are you thinking of moving back home?" She took a sip of her drink.

"I don't know. Maybe I'll find a roommate and get a bigger place. My dad and I don't get along so well."

She knew that.

"To be honest, Brian, I've been lonely, too."

He gave her a sideways glance. "We could do something about that."

When she made no reply, he gently pressed his index finger beneath her chin and lifted her mouth toward his. "Would you mind…?"

When she gazed at his lips and didn't object, he pressed his mouth to hers.

The following morning, Denise found herself in Brian's bed and mentally berated herself again. She told herself that she was the most pathetic, desperate loser on the planet, and she'd only made her situation with Brian worse by using him. Now, he would expect to see her again.

As she gathered her clothes from the floor, he offered her a bowl of cereal, but she said she just wanted to get home, so, once they'd dressed, he took her down the street to her car at Whataburger, where he said he'd call her.

Her father didn't say anything to her when she walked in, but she could tell he'd been worried.

"I'm sorry I didn't tell you where I was," she said.

"A simple phone call, Denise. That's all I need. You're an adult, but you live with me, and I worry when I don't know where you are."

"I'm sorry, Daddy. It won't happen again."

She went to her room and fell onto her bed. Then, on impulse, she opened her laptop, returned to the genealogy website, and typed: *Markos Nadir, 2014, New York, New York.*

A single link appeared in the search results, along with the message: *View records for Markos Nadir with your 14-day free trial.*

With her heart pounding in her throat, she clicked on the link. After signing up for a free trial with a credit card, she gained access to the record. It listed Markos Ari Nadir, born November 30, 2014. The record included the names of each parent—Ammon and Eboni—and a street address.

Denise took a deep breath. *A street address.*

The following Tuesday, as she was adding new extensions to Lucinda's hair, Denise asked her friend if she'd be interested in a weekend girls' trip to New York City.

"I love New York," Lucinda said. "It's my favorite city."

"You've been?"

"Three times. Once with my aunt, once with my mom, and once with Ronnie."

Ronnie was her boyfriend.

"Want to go with me?" Denise asked. "If I can afford it, I mean?"

"When?"

"Next month? After final exams?"

"We need to book our flight now," Lucinda said. "The earlier we book, the better the deal."

Denise smiled. "So, is that a yes?"

"That's a yes, girlfriend!" Then she added, "We can stay with my mom's cousin, Margo. That's where we always stay when we go."

"Then I'mma do your hair for free!" Denise said with a gleeful smile.

Between the flight and the cab fares, Denise would not have been able to afford the weekend trip to New York City if her friend hadn't offered her a place to stay. Lucinda had wanted to show off what she knew by taking Denise to a Broadway production, to Ellis Island, to the Empire

State Building, and to the other touristy things, but Denise couldn't afford them.

"I'm not your regular tourist," Denise said. "I'm here for the culture. I just want to walk through Korean Town and eat me some good Korean food."

"The least you can do is see Central Park and go shopping with me at Rockefeller Center," Lucinda insisted.

Denise yielded, and they spent Saturday afternoon shopping all through Rockefeller Center and then took a cab to Central Park, where they walked around, eating hot dogs and sipping sodas. Lucinda showed her the fountain featured in the opening of the sitcom *Friends* and then took her to a terrace to see the ornate Minton tile ceiling beneath the bridge. As they stood beneath the majesty of the incredibly detailed work overhead, Denise had the urge to confide in Lucinda about why she'd really wanted to come to New York.

"Lucinda," she began. "There's something I need to tell you, and it's going to sound a little crazy."

Once Denise had begun the story of Markos Nadir, she hadn't been able to stop until every detail had been told. Lucinda sat beside her on a bench in Central Park, taking it all in with wide eyes.

"I know he must have been sick, like my father," Denise said when she had finished. "He created the whole time-travel fantasy as a coping mechanism, I'm sure, but…"

"But what?" Lucinda asked.

Denise clutched the sapphire pendant that hung between her breasts. "Do you think it's remotely possible that he could have been telling the truth?"

Lucinda laughed. "Yeah, I don't think so. I just can't believe he put you through all of that. You could have died."

Denise heaved a heavy sigh. "That's what I think, too, but…" She took a folded piece of paper from her purse. "I feel it's only right that I prove it, you know? I need to prove that it was delusion, so I can have peace of mind and move on."

"And what's that?" Lucinda asked, pointing to the paper.

"It's the address of a family who have a three-year-old named Markos Nadir."

Lucinda narrowed her eyes. "What will that prove? There could be tons of people named Markos Nadir, especially in New York."

"Markos told me his parents were from Egypt," Denise said. "How likely could it be that there was a Markos Nadir born in New York City around the time he claims to have been born by parents who immigrated here from Egypt?"

Lucinda lifted her palms. "Who knows? What will it prove?"

"If the parents *aren't* from Egypt, then I can move on," Denise insisted.

"And if they are?"

Denise shrugged. "Then I need to search for more proof."

Lucinda agreed to take the hour-long bus ride from Central Park to Brooklyn to find the address Denise had on the folded paper in her pocket. During the ride, Lucinda asked Denise questions about her time on the yacht.

"Did you really fall in love with him?" Lucinda asked. "It seemed real to you?"

Denise nodded. "I still love him. Even after everything. Don't you see? That's why I have to rule out the possibility that he might have been telling the truth, however hard it is to believe."

"Even if the parents are from Egypt, that won't mean…"

"I know," Denise said.

"So, what will you do?"

Denise replied, "I don't know."

When the bus finally dropped them at the corner of Bay Ridge and Fourth Avenue, they walked the streets to 7159 Ridge Boulevard and found a cute house that had been converted into apartments. The online record hadn't given Denise an apartment number, so she had no idea which door she should knock on first.

As she stood there on the sidewalk with her friend beneath the ever-darkening sky, a man stepped out onto the upstairs balcony to smoke a cigarette.

Without thinking, Denise asked, "Excuse me. Are you Mr. Nadir?"

"No," the young man said. "He lives next door."

"Do you know if he and his wife are from Egypt?" Lucinda blurted out.

"Yes, why?" he asked.

"Yes, you know, or yes, they're from Egypt?" Denise asked.

"Both," he said with a laugh.

Lucinda turned to Denise and said, "So much for ruling that out."

"I want to see the boy," Denise whispered to Lucinda.

"What? Are you crazy?" Lucinda whispered back. "What family is going to let some strange girl look at their child for no apparent reason."

To the man on the balcony, Denise said, "I heard that they want to hire a nanny, for their son, Markos. I know it's late, but do you think they might still be awake?"

"Ammon will come out soon," the man said. "He always has a smoke around this time, too. You can ask him."

"Come on, Denise," Lucinda whispered. "This is crazy. Let's get out of here."

"Speak of the devil," the man on the balcony said. "Ammon, these beautiful girls are here to see you."

Not much light illuminated the balcony from the evening sky, but a streetlamp was enough for Denise to see that Ammon's eyes were black, as were the rest of his features.

"Stop your lying, my friend," Ammon said. "I won't cover for you if you get in trouble with your wife."

"Come on, man, I'm speaking the truth. They want to be Markos's nanny."

"I heard you were looking for one," Denise said. "I'm sorry if this is a bad time."

"My wife didn't say anything about it to me," Ammon said, "but what do I know? Let me get her." He stuck his head in the door and called, "Eboni! There's someone here to see you!"

Denise prayed that the woman would bring her son, so that Denise could have a look at him. It was one thing for there to be another Markos Nadir born in New York to Egyptian immigrants around the time Markos claimed to be born; it was another thing entirely if that boy also possessed the same supremely brilliant emerald eyes.

The woman stepped out onto the balcony without her son, and disappointment overwhelmed Denise. She resisted the urge to ask to see the boy.

"Over there," Ammon pointed down to Denise and Lucinda. "They said you're looking for a nanny for Markos."

The woman turned her face down to look at the girls on the sidewalk, and Denise's mouth fell open.

"I'm sorry," the woman said. "But you have wrong information. I don't need a nanny. Where did you hear otherwise?"

Beneath the light of the streetlamp, Eboni's emerald eyes blazed with beauty, equal to that of Markos's.

Denise was speechless.

"Our mistake," Lucinda said. "We must have the wrong address." Then to Denise, she said, "Come on. Let's go."

CHAPTER SEVENTEEN

Third Sign

The summer after her freshman year at Trinity, Denise could not give up her search for Markos. She called and texted his phone repeatedly, to no avail. She found his address and visited his apartment but found it vacant. She went in person and questioned the chair of the Physics Department, hoping for a forwarding address, and she conducted Google searches daily—sometimes more than once a day. But her efforts were futile. There seemed to be no lead in San Antonio or on the Internet, which meant only one thing: she needed to return to Apra Harbor, Guam to *The Mariela*.

It took all summer for her to earn enough money for a roundtrip flight. Her father tried to talk her out of it. Lucinda tried to talk her out of it. Even Aunt Latisha pulled her aside one Sunday and said, "What's wrong with you?"

But there was nothing anyone could say. Denise had to prove Markos wrong, or she couldn't move on.

In mid-August, a week before her fall semester would begin, Denise flew to Guam. Her flight itinerary traced the same path she'd taken with Markos: Los Angeles, Honolulu, and, finally, Guam International Airport. Over twenty-four hours had passed from the time she had boarded in San Antonio to the time she was in a cab on her way to Apra Harbor.

The driver took her past the naval ships to the private marina on the southside of the harbor where Markos had last docked *The Mariela*.

"I'll be right back," she told the driver.

Denise stepped out of the cab into the hot, windy day and ran across the street to the docks. There were about a dozen ships nestled together. Denise inspected each one, but she did not find *The Mariela* among them.

If Markos's ship wasn't here, where he usually docked it, then maybe he'd sailed to the Mariana Trench. Her heart filled with joy at the possibility of finding him. She rode the cab to her hotel room, and, after checking in, used her phone to charter a boat for the next day.

The catamaran sailed across the Pacific Ocean from Apra Harbor early the next morning with a Filipino captain named Zenji and Denise on board. The sky was clear, but the sea was far from calm, and the wind railed against Denise's face as she searched the horizon for *The Mariela*.

The captain was younger than she had expected—maybe five years her senior—and not very talkative. He had a clean-shaven, baby face, round eyes, and a soft-spoken voice. He sat in the cockpit above where she stood on deck of the bow, gripping the rail.

Grateful that Zenji accepted credit cards, Denise tried not to think about the tremendous amount of money she'd poured into this adventure, reminding herself that she needed closure and wouldn't get it unless she could prove that Markos had, indeed, been delusional. If there was even a smidgen of a possibility that he'd been telling the truth, she had to know.

All that money would be wasted if she did not find him. He could have sailed anywhere in the world. Would she charter boats to search the ends of the earth to find him?

For over two hours, Denise stood in her life-vest clinging to the rail of the catamaran, looking in a single direction—east—toward the Marianas, when the appearance of a solitary ship anchored in the distance sparked a flame of hope.

"There!" she cried to the captain.

As the catamaran slowed and approached the yacht—same shape, same size, same color as the one owned by Markos—Denise waited for the name of the ship to come into view and gasped when she read: *The Mariela.*

"This is it!" she shouted to Zenji. And then, scanning the cockpit and deck of the yacht, but seeing no one aboard, she cried, "Markos! Markos!"

When Markos didn't appear, she turned to the captain and said, "He must be below. Please, help me aboard!"

Zenji climbed down from the cockpit and tied onto the yacht as Denise strained her eyes, hoping to catch a glimpse of Markos in the kitchen or salon through the windows. Once they were tied, Zenji offered Denise a hand, and she climbed over the rail of the catamaran and onto the deck of *The Mariela.*

"Markos?" She ran through the salon, just to be sure he hadn't been lying on the couch, and then not finding him there, she scurried down the steps to the hull.

First, she hurried to his cabin and knocked on the door. "Markos?"

Finding the door unlocked, she opened it. The bed was empty and unmade. A pair of trousers were lying on the floor where he must have stepped out of them. She scooped the trousers in her arms and hugged them before tossing them onto the bed. In the bathroom, she found a towel hanging over the rod of the shower. She pressed the towel against her face. Although the towel was dry, she could smell Markos's scent.

She rushed from his cabin to the engineering room, hoping to find him at work on the sub, but when she made her way past the engine and equipment, she found the submarine gone.

She bolted up to the deck. The captain was waiting for her on the catamaran.

"He's taken the sub," she shouted. "I want to wait for him."

"How long?" Zenji asked.

"However long it takes."

"You'll ring up a mighty high tab if you keep me here for more than a day."

Tears flooded her eyes. "I don't care. I don't care! I'll pay you however much you want!"

Zenji looked away, as if he was embarrassed by her outburst. But a moment later, he turned to her and said, "Listen. I have to come this way in a few days for another client. Let's go back now, and I won't charge you for the return trip out here. What do you say?"

"Leave me here," she said. "And when you come back, I'll return with you, if Markos hasn't shown up by then."

"Leave you here? Alone at sea?" Zenji shook his head. "Not a good idea."

"I'll be fine," she insisted. "I have the radio if I need help."

"I could lose my license," he said.

"I won't tell anyone."

"And if something happens to you?"

"Nothing's going to happen to me. You said there's no bad weather in the forecast."

"You can't count on the forecast."

"Please, Zenji. Unless you pick me up and carry me, I'm staying here."

Zenji climbed over the rail of the catamaran and boarded *The Mariela*. "I'll only consider this if you have enough food and supplies. And I need to make sure the radio works."

She followed Zenji to the kitchen, where he opened the fridge and cabinets and found canned goods, fresh water, and a few other non-perishable items. The fact that Markos had no fresh foods on hand didn't necessarily mean he'd been gone long. He'd told her last March that he usually ate canned food while on the yacht.

Next, she followed the captain to the cockpit, where he turned on the radio and, said, into the receiver, "Testing, testing. Anybody read me? Over."

There was nothing but static, so the captain repeated, "Testing, testing. This is the captain of *The Caraballa.* Anybody read me? Over."

"Hello, Zenji," came a voice over the radio. "This is Anthony. I read you loud and clear. Over."

"Salamat, kaibigan," Zenji said before turning off the radio. Then he turned to Denise. "I'll be back in three days. If you need me before then, use the radio. Got it?"

She threw her arms around his neck, which caused him to blush severely.

"Thank you!" she cried as she pulled away. "Thank you so much!"

For most of the day, Denise sat on the upper deck with her eyes on the sea, turning to look in all directions, as she hoped the submarine would breach the surface and bring Markos back. It wasn't that she believed his story; she still couldn't take that leap of faith. His tale of time-travel and of parallel worlds had been too fantastical and difficult to imagine, especially since no one else on earth had claimed to experience anything like it.

Nevertheless, she missed him terribly. She'd been wrong to let him go. If she had remained in his life, she might have convinced him, over time, to let go of the fantasy and to live in the present.

Adding to her desperation to see Markos was the eerie resemblance of Eboni Nadir's emerald-green eyes to his.

When night fell, and she could no longer see the ocean beyond the lights cast by the yacht, Denise found a can of corn and ate in the salon. She suffered from the agonizing fear that Markos was dead at the bottom of the sea, and she needed a distraction. When she turned on the television, she was surprised it worked, because she and Markos hadn't watched it a single time over Spring Break. She surfed through the channels and found three stations, but only one was in English. The English program was a baseball game, and, since she had no interest, she turned off the television and went downstairs to Markos's cabin.

With tears in her eyes, she took off her clothes and lay between his sheets, imagining the places where his body must have also touched them. She replayed their one night together on the upper deck over and over in her mind and pressed her nose into his pillow and inhaled his musky scent.

The room was dark and lonely, so she turned on the bedside lamp and searched his top drawer for something to read. Expecting to find a book or a magazine, she was surprised to find a handwritten letter.

Dear Dee,

It's been three years since I traveled back in time from 2040. Here, in 2018, in the month of March, I've left this letter knowing you would look for it, if you found my ship.

I've gone to the interdimensional portal to continue my search for a place where time-travel forward is possible, but not because I have yet to save Mariela. Your "past you" will see to her survival by getting her to a doctor before her seventeenth birthday.

I understand that I have changed the future, so things will be different when I return. I am also different. During my visit to the past, something not entirely unexpected has happened. I've fallen in love with your younger self.

Please don't be repulsed by that news. We've always had a strong connection, and, after Mariela's death, you were my greatest comfort.

In meeting and getting to know the "past you," I've come to believe that, while we both loved Mariela, you and I are soulmates.

I couldn't convince the "past you" to believe me. You broke my heart, Dee. Now, I'm in search of you, hoping to convince you to forget our age difference and end our mutual loneliness by being together.

If I don't succeed in finding you, I'll return to this ship. If you read this letter but don't wish to wait for me, then leave me word where you used to drop your letters on our first ship, in the drawer of your bedside table.

Yours Truly,

M

Denise reread the letter, wondering, first, if they were the rantings of a mad man, and, second, if "Dee" referred to her. Her brother used to call her "Dee" but hadn't in many years—not since their mother had died.

Her third thought was that Markos had been gone since he left the university in March. That was over four months ago. Surely, he couldn't still be somewhere in the depths of the Mariana Trench and be alive. Perhaps he'd returned since leaving the letter. Denise could only hope.

Her fourth thought was to look in the drawer of the bedside table in the cabin where she had slept during Spring Break.

Not that she expected to find anything, of course. Of course, she didn't. Without bothering to dress, she left Markos's cabin and headed for the room down the hall.

When she entered the room, she found the bed unmade, though she had made it the last time she'd been here. Had he slept in it, thinking of her, before he'd left in the submarine? As she crossed the room to the bedside table, she remembered to breathe, but her knees nearly buckled beneath her when she opened the drawer and found a letter addressed to her *in her own writing.*

Dear Denise,
I'm from your future.

Denise's hands began to tremble as her mouth dropped open. She fell on the bed, unable to stand, as she continued reading the letter.

Markos has told you the truth. He's the love of your life. Don't ever stop looking for him.
Yours Truly,
"Dee"

Denise reread the letter with one hand over her mouth. Then she read it again. Had it really been written by *her*—a *future her?*

She fell back on the bed, clutching her heart.

The letter was in her own handwriting.

Markos had told her the truth.

Over the next few days, while she waited for Zenji's return, Denise grappled with the truth of all that had happened and struggled to compose a letter of her own, which she would leave beside "Dee's" in the bedside drawer. She drafted at least a dozen of them before she settled on this:

My Sweet Markos,

Today is August 12, 2018. I was your student last fall, to whom you taught the principles of gravitational lensing, the shimmering effect, and closed time-like curves. I've spent the last few months searching for you, because it was a mistake to let you go.

Please come back to me, Markos. I'm so sorry I didn't believe you, but I do now. I also believe that what you once said is true: we're soulmates. I'm the love of your life, as you are mine.

With All My Love,

Denise

CHAPTER EIGHTEEN

Markos Nadir

Denise continued her desperate search for Markos. Before graduating with her bachelor's degree in physics in 2021, she'd made three more trips to Guam and to *The Mariela*. Each time, she found the ship exactly as she'd left it, except for the wear and tear of age, with no sign of Markos or her future self.

In her desperation to find him, she studied the space-time continuum and discovered a break-through equation proving that objects had the potential to travel faster than light. Her paper was published and noticed by Harvard University, which offered her a scholarship to continue her studies there. At Harvard, she focused on closed time-like curves and, after completing a dissertation on that topic that received international recognition, she accepted a job working for NASA at the Johnson Space Center in Houston, Texas in 2027.

She'd made four more trips to *The Mariela* before her time at Harvard had ended, and there was still no sign of Markos.

Denise also made annual trips to New York City to spy on Markos's younger self until the Nadir family moved in 2026, and she lost track of them.

At NASA, she joined a team devoted to finding ways to manipulate the fabric of space-time using nuclear energy. Influenced by the story Markos had shared with her years before, Denise steered the team in the direction of creating an underwater vessel that might eventually travel to the Mariana Trench to rip a hole in the space-time continuum.

There were countless nights when she lay in bed in her lonely apartment in Houston, weeping for the life she might have had with Markos if she'd only believed him that March of 2018. She'd twist her blankets, toss and turn, bite the inside of her lips, and cry until she had no more tears to shed, no more energy to move, and she would fall asleep, at last, only to dream of him.

It was her fervent desire to find a world where time-travel was possible so she could go back in time to find him. With that second chance, she would believe him. With that second chance, they'd stay together.

By 2033, her team at NASA had conducted two preliminary underwater launches of the submarine they'd designed for interdimensional travel. That was also the year that Denise fulfilled her promise to Markos by taking her niece Mariela to see an oncologist. Pre-cancerous tumors were discovered and treated the same year.

Three years later, in early autumn, Mariela called Denise, where she'd been working in her lab.

"Hi, Auntie Dee," Mariela said. "I know you're busy, but I want to invite you to Grandpa's this Sunday for lunch. I want you to meet my boyfriend."

Denise couldn't breathe.

"Auntie Dee? You there?"

"I'm, here, Mariela." Denise sat in a chair and held up five fingers to the other members of her team—a gesture they understood to mean, *Take five minutes.*

"So, can you come for lunch on Sunday?" Mariela asked again.

"This guy must be pretty special, huh?" Denise asked.

"He sure is. I really think you're gonna like him."

"What's his name?" Denise held her breath.

"Markos. He's a doctor—well, an intern. And he's so nice and smart and handsome. I can't believe he likes me!"

"I'm looking forward to meeting him, then," Denise said. "What should I bring?"

"You don't have to bring anything. Just your presence will be a gift!"

"Oh, honey, you're sweet, but I want to bring something. Maybe a dessert?"

"How about your famous lemon cream cake. I've already told him it's my favorite."

Denise's eyes were moist. "Okay, honey. You got it. I'll see you on Sunday."

Denise drove to San Antonio Saturday evening, to spend time with her father, his wife Cherie, and their son Tyrese, who, earlier that month, had turned twelve years old. Now that her father had retired from his eighteen-year position teaching high-school biology, he seemed to forget how busy working folk can be and expected Denise to visit more frequently. She tried to make their Sunday family dinners once a month, and, if she missed a month due to work, she got an earful from her father about the importance of family.

But what her father didn't understand was that her heart's family wasn't complete. If Markos was still alive, she had to find him, no matter how long it took. Her team at NASA was nearly ready to make its first launch to the deepest region of the Mariana Trench to try their hand at ripping space-time.

While she visited with her family, Denise baked her lemon cream cake, recalling the first time she'd ever made it and how Markos had referred to it as "famous." She wondered now how many times he'd eaten it before that day.

When Sunday afternoon finally arrived, Denise was shaking with anticipation. Cherie had cooked a pan of roasted chicken and rice, and her father had chopped vegetables for a salad. Denise played a video game on the XBOX with Tyrese to distract herself from the fact that she was about to meet Markos Nadir.

The doorbell rang, and Denise froze.

"Dee, how'd you miss that shot!" Tyrese complained of the game. "Now you're dead!"

"Sorry," she said, climbing to her feet as her father opened the front door.

It was Aunt Latisha.

"I hope fruit salad sounds good," she said as she carried a bowl covered in plastic wrap into the kitchen. "Well, hello, Denise! I didn't know you'd be here today! That's two times in one month. Aren't we lucky!"

Denise hugged her aunt. "Mariela asked me to come and meet her new beaux."

"Speaking of which," Aunt Latisha said. "Did you know he has the exact same name as that professor you dated your freshman year at Trinity? Markos Nadir, wasn't it?"

Denise frowned as a shiver worked down her spine. Forcing a smile, she said, "Yes. Isn't that something?"

"I guess it's not an uncommon name," Cherie said from the kitchen.

"I wonder whatever happened to your young man," Aunt Latisha said. "I thought he was going to marry you, Dee."

Denise forced another smile and then excused herself to the restroom.

Once behind the closed door, she turned on the water at the bathroom sink and splashed a bit of cold water onto her cheeks. She was burning up and felt as if she was about to faint.

Then she heard the doorbell. As she stared at her reflection in the mirror over the sink, she saw the blood leave her face. Within a few seconds, her body went from burning up to cool and clammy. The room started spinning. Then she lifted the lid on the commode and was sick.

She spent several minutes cleaning up, rinsing her mouth, and deodorizing the room when there was a knock on the bathroom door.

"You alright in there, Baby?" came her father's voice.

"I'll be right out, Daddy" she said.

Without allowing herself to think about it, she opened the door and walked into the living room, where Mariela was introducing her boyfriend to the family. Markos Nadir turned and looked at Denise as soon as she entered.

"Hello," he said to her. "Do I know you?"

Denise couldn't breathe. He appeared exactly as he had nineteen years ago when he'd walked into her Introduction to Physics class her freshman year. His beautiful features—smooth dark skin, short curly hair, square jaw, thick lips, and, most importantly, those supremely beautiful emerald eyes looked exactly as she remembered them.

"This is my Auntie Dee," Mariela said. "Auntie Dee, this is Markos."

He reached out to shake her hand, but Denise couldn't move.

"Is it me, or is this young man the spitting image of the one you brought home twenty years ago?" Aunt Latisha said.

"Excuse me?" Markos turned a perplexed face to Mariela. "What's going on?"

"That's exactly what I thought," Kassia said with a laugh. "Didn't I, Girard?"

"That's a fact," Girard said. "Maybe they're related somehow."

Denise snapped out of her stunned silence and gave a nervous laugh. To Markos, she said, "You look like a boy I dated once. That's all." She laughed again.

"I guess we both have good taste in men," Mariela said with a feisty grin.

Everyone in the room laughed except for Tyrese, who groaned, "Please!"

"It's nice to meet you, Auntie Dee." Markos reached his hand out to her again.

When she took his hand in hers, tears pricked her eyes. It felt amazing to touch him, and a flood of memories of all the moments he'd caressed her, kissed her, and gazed into her eyes overwhelmed her. She let go of his hand, quickly, and rushed to the table.

"Shall we eat?" she asked, batting the tears from her eyes and forcing yet another smile.

The rest of her family joined her at the table, where her father said a blessing before Cherie passed the first of the dishes to Markos, since he was their guest.

Throughout the meal, Denise couldn't peel her eyes away from Markos. His mannerisms, his voice, and his features haunted her, and she couldn't stop her eyes from filling with tears. She dabbed her eyes with a napkin and blamed it on allergies.

She was reminded of the first time she'd brought Markos home and he'd met Mariela as a baby. She could now imagine the pain he'd felt as he held her and realized he would never be with her the way he'd once imagined he would. Denise had a similar epiphany as she watched her niece and young Markos. Even if Denise could find a way back in time to that first semester of her freshman year, she would be aged, and Markos would still be a young man of twenty-eight. He wouldn't have yet fallen in love with her, and there was little chance of that happening with the forty-something version she would be by the time she found him.

That night, after everyone had left and she was alone in her room, she wept in her bed, trying to come to terms with the fact that she had to let go of her dream of being with Markos. For the hundredth time, she reminded herself that, for all she knew, he could dead, a corpse in his sub, at the bottom of the Mariana Trench.

Maybe one day, when she took her own sub to those ocean depths, she would find him and bury him, once and for all.

Since she couldn't sleep, she did what she often did during her visits to San Antonio when she was feeling lonely and blue, she called Brian Jameson.

Over a year later, while the Christmas decorations still adorned the chapel at First Baptist Church on Lockwood Street, Denise stood in a pew beside her father on a Saturday afternoon, witnessing the marriage of Mariela to Markos Nadir. Denise held onto her father's arm while the pastor congratulated the bride and groom, because she could barely stand without it, and, as tears streamed down her cheeks, she hoped everyone around her believed they were tears of happiness.

Denise *was* happy for her sweet Mariela, but she was simultaneously tormented by the agony of seeing the man she loved marry someone else. What was worse, that man had no knowledge of how deeply he'd once loved Denise.

Over a year ago, when Mariela had first brought her new beaux to the family's Sunday dinner, Denise had come to terms with living a life without Markos; but today's ceremony felt like the sharp stab of finality that drove the blade through Denise's heart and destroyed her.

After photographs of the bride and groom and their families and wedding party had been taken in front of the church, everyone was told to proceed to the hall for the punch and cake reception. Denise clung to her father's arm as they walked across the church grounds against the bitter cold. The leaves of the giant red oak between the two buildings had been falling for months and continued to fall to cover the grass and sidewalk. One of them blew up toward her face and caught itself in her hair. Her father noticed it, plucked it out for her, and handed it over. She laughed, hiding her pain, and held it like a delicate flower as they entered the decorated foyer.

Denise stood in line by the bride's framed portrait, looking lovely on an easel, to sign the guest registry. Then she followed the other family and friends into the main hall. The beautiful couple stood in the center of the room near the cake surrounded by their guests. The best man held his champagne flute and delivered a toast. The bride and groom cut the cake and fed one another. Then guests were asked to celebrate by joining the couple for cake and punch.

Denise couldn't eat, but she helped herself to more champagne and drank a fifth glass down where she stood in a corner near the ladies' room, alone. There were plenty of people in the hall with whom she could share a table and a conversation, but she wanted, more than anything, to be left alone so that she could come to terms with the death of a dream. For Denise, today wasn't just a wedding; it was also a funeral, and she needed to grieve.

As she stood there, drowning her sorrows with the delicate champagne flute, she spotted someone unknown and yet familiar standing in the corner by the men's room opposite her. Like her, he seemed to have intentionally separated himself from the other guests, wanting and not wanting to be among them. He wore a long dark coat over his suit, with the collar turned up, and a fedora pulled down over his brow. He hadn't noticed her observing him, for he was preoccupied with the bride and groom.

He held his glass near his mouth, which blocked her view of his face. He seemed to be a relative of the groom's—perhaps an uncle, or maybe even the father of the groom. But when the man dropped his arm to his side, revealing his face, Denise's champagne flute fell from her hand and shattered on the wooden floor.

The man standing across from her was Markos Nadir—not Markos the young groom, but *her* Markos.

<u>CHAPTER NINETEEN</u>

Futility

"Markos?" Denise took a step toward him.

When his eyes met hers, his mouth fell open, and he staggered back.

"You must have me confused with someone else," he muttered before he crossed the room toward the exit.

"Markos, wait!" Denise followed him through the crowd of wedding guests, through the foyer with the bridal portrait, and out into the bitter cold, past the huge red oak and its falling leaves. "Please, Markos!"

He froze near the parking lot with his back to her, as if he'd been turned into a pillar of stone. She ran to him but stopped short, about three feet away from him.

"Is it really you?" she asked, as tears flooded her eyes and streamed down her cheeks.

Slowly, he turned to face her. She took another step toward him and peered up at him beneath the afternoon sun. Although, like her, he'd aged, his supremely beautiful emerald eyes were no less extraordinary.

"Markos!" she threw her arms around his neck.

He stiffened beneath her.

She pulled back and studied his face. "What's wrong?"

When he still hadn't uttered a word, she said, through chattering teeth, "I've searched for you for years. Where have you been?"

Although he said nothing, his lips trembled, and tears filled his eyes.

"Please say something."

He took a deep breath and sucked in his lips. In a broken voice, he said, "You look beautiful."

"Oh, Markos!"

Once again, she embraced him, and this time, his arms wrapped around her waist and pulled her against him, like a vice. He pressed his mouth against hers, his lips ravaging hers, his hands cupping her head and pressing her closer, closer.

He pulled away. "I can't!"

Her heart felt as if it had been ripped from her chest. She stood there before him, trembling and dizzy. A sharp pain seared through her gut as she wondered if he'd married another. "Why not?"

He took a handkerchief from his pocket and handed it to her. "Why didn't you go on with your life? Aren't you married by now?"

For a horrifying moment, her knees buckled, and she nearly fainted. He caught her in his arms and steadied her.

"Did *you*, Markos? Did *you* go on with your life?"

"Oh, Denise."

With trembling hands, she dabbed her eyes with his handkerchief, breathing in his scent. "You did, didn't you? You married another."

"No," he said. "I never married, not since Mariela died."

Her mouth fell open as hope bloomed in her chest. "Then what's wrong, Markos? What's holding you back?"

"We need to talk. Not here. Let's go somewhere private."

"I can't just leave Mariela's wedding," she said.

"I shouldn't have come," he said. "I couldn't help myself."

"Why *did* you come?" she asked, angered by his cryptic behavior.

"I was sure you'd moved on. I didn't think you'd expect to see me, didn't think you'd notice me."

Panting now with rage, she clenched her teeth and balled her fists.

"I'm sorry," he said.

"I've searched for you for twenty years," she said through her clenched teeth. "I've lost count of the number of times I've sailed out to *The Mariela*, hoping you'd returned."

"What?"

"I've spent years trying to understand the fabric of space-time, entertaining the idea of going back, to when we first met."

"Denise, I…"

"I've built a tachyonic cannon for the purpose of ripping space-time, Markos. I've fought for grants and private funding to build a vessel that might withstand interdimensional travel, to search every possible world for you."

He stepped toward her and put his hands on her shoulders. "Denise…"

"So, don't stand there and tell me that you didn't think I'd notice you. Of course, I noticed you. I've devoted every minute of my life, since you left, to finding you."

He gazed at her mouth, his features twisted with agony. Unable to stop herself, she pressed her lips to his.

Again, he ravaged her, as if unleashing twenty years' worth of passion and longing. She fell against him, unable to stand.

"Let's get out of here," he whispered. "Did you drive?"

"I rode with my father." She used the stylist on her wristlet to text her father. "I'll let him know I took a cab home. I'll say I wasn't feeling well."

"Is that the digital wristlet I gave you years ago?" he asked.

"Yeah, it is," she said with a half-smile. "I know it's ancient compared to what everyone's using these days, but I couldn't bring myself to part with it. And it works, so…"

"And you still wear the sapphire pendant," he said, taking the stone between his fingers before letting it fall to rest between her breasts.

"Where should we go?" she asked, full of longing.

"My hotel," he said. "If that's okay with you. We can talk there."

She hoped they would do more than talk as he led her to through the parking lot.

"Is this yours, or a rental?" she asked, once they were inside the black sedan.

"A rental." He pulled from the parking lot.

"Where do you live?"

"On another world, in what we call Sector 109." He took the ramp onto the highway toward downtown.

"Why? Why there?"

"It's the most advanced world I've discovered so far," he explained. "About every five years, I return with medicines and technologies, to help our world."

"How very noble of you."

He sighed.

"I suppose you never found my letter."

He gave her a sideways glance. "No. What letter?"

"I left it in my bedside drawer on *The Mariela*."

He exited the highway toward the Riverwalk. "I haven't been aboard that ship in ages."

She furrowed her brows. "What? Then how do you travel?"

"I was introduced to another interdimensional portal by a group of scientists at Sector 109. It's more accessible, up at the brink of our atmosphere, over the North Pole. I travel by private jet."

"Oh."

He pulled into the parking garage of the Marriot Hotel and searched for a place to park the car.

Once he'd parked, he turned to her and said, "I never meant to hurt you, Denise."

She couldn't meet his eyes. Her stomach was churning, and she was spinning, spinning.

"I intended to do the exact opposite," he said. "I hope you believe me. I hope you know that I never stopped loving you. I stayed away for your sake, not mine."

She threw her head back and looked down her nose at him. "My sake? How so?"

He unbuckled his safety strap. "Let's go inside."

He led her through the hotel lobby to an elevator. They rode it to the penthouse suite, where he turned on the gas fireplace, helped her out of her coat, and offered her one of two wingback chairs.

As she took her seat, he gave her a once-over before asking, "Can I get you a glass of wine?"

"Yes, please." She needed it more than ever.

He removed his coat and fedora, and his suit jacket and tie, and un-buttoned the top button of his white shirt. She couldn't peel her eyes away. Was this really *her* Markos standing in the same room with her, or was she dreaming? With trembling hands, he poured them each of glass of wine. He handed her one and sat in the other chair, across from her.

"Thank you," she said of the wine before taking a sip. It was deli-cious.

"My pleasure, Denise. I can't believe we're sitting here together. I can hardly believe my eyes."

"Where have you been?"

He drained his glass and leaned back in the chair, crossing one ankle over his knee. It reminded her of how he used to sit behind his desk in his office at Trinity, years ago.

"After we returned from our trip to the Mariana Trench that Spring Break of 2018, I left this world to return to Sector 22, the place where I had traveled in time from 2040."

"To look for *future me*, right?"

His eyes widened. "Yes. How did you know?"

"I found the letter you left for her in your bedside drawer on *The Mariela*."

"The technology to travel forward had still not been developed there. I searched the worlds for a way forward in time but gave up after four or five years."

"She left a letter for me, too. Did you know that?" Denise asked.

His mouth fell open. "What? No? She came back in time?"

"Yes. She told me to never stop looking for you."

"She was time-traveling, all that time. No wonder." He got up and poured himself another glass of wine with a very shaky hand.

"So, you never found her?"

He shook his head.

"I returned to Sector 22, where I was recognized by a fellow time-traveler, a very old woman who knew my name."

"Who was she?" she asked.

"I'd never seen her before in my life."

"But she knew you?" She took another sip of wine.

"She invited me to a restaurant so we could exchange our stories and discuss our mutual fascination with time travel. Eventually, she admitted that she was an expert on causal loops."

"An expert? In what way?"

"She followed case studies and documented them. She'd been studying me—us. According to her, you and I have been part of an ongoing causal loop for most of her lifetime. I'd actually suspected as much."

"How is that possible?" Denise asked.

"Her world—Sector 200—has what are called seers, and she's one of them. They're capable of utilizing parts of their brains that are inaccessible to people on most worlds. They can see all of time at once."

"I don't understand."

"If all time exists already, and our consciousness merely travels from one space to the next to experience time, imagine if you could train yourself to experience all moments at once."

Denise leaned forward in her seat. "That's so difficult to comprehend."

"The old woman told me that…" his voice broke off and he covered his mouth as he fought tears.

Denise set down the glass of wine and went down on her knees, gripping his ankle. "Told you what, Markos?"

He sat forward and cupped her face. "The loop can't be broken."

She covered his trembling hands with her own, realizing for the first time what he'd been trying to say. Everything had always played out the same way. Nothing had changed. Nothing would change.

"When we ensured Mariela's survival, there was no longer a reason for you to send me back in time to save her," he said. "And the moment I no longer traveled back in time, I—the time-traveler—ceased to exist."

"But you do exist. I can see you, feel you. You're sitting here before my eyes."

"According to the old woman, when that younger version of myself we saw today at the First Baptist Church on Lockwood Street, the one who just married Mariela, does *not* travel back in time in his year 2040, I will disappear from the timeline."

Denise fell back, on her bottom and hugged her knees to her chest, trying to piece it all together. "But if you disappear, won't the technologies and medicines and everything you brought back…"

"And Mariela dies, as she always has, and always will."

"No." Denise covered her mouth.

"And you'll lose all memories of our time together, as if I'd never existed."

She shook her head, fervently. "No!"

"And just before Mariela dies, you'll convince her husband to travel back in time, just as you've always done and will always do."

Denise could barely breathe as she sat there, wide-eyed, mouth hanging open. "It will start all over again."

"That's what the old woman wanted to tell me," he said. "There's no way out of the loop."

Denise sat in stunned silence, taking it all in. There was no changing time. Everything that was ever to happen had always happened. Every move she made was the move she'd always made, on every point of the timeline. Going back did nothing. Whatever she experienced was all experience.

"But you'll continue to exist in that closed loop, won't you?" she asked.

"Yes, I always have and always will. This little time aberration is where you and I have our moments together. Even though you won't remember them, they will always exist."

"I don't understand why you didn't come back to me before now," she finally said. "We could have had *twenty-three* years together."

He bent his brows. "When I last left you, you wanted nothing to do with me."

"Surely you understand why," she said.

"Your father was cured, I'd warned you about Brian, and there was no reason why you couldn't marry, have children, and live happily ever after. I wanted that for you."

"There *was* a reason I couldn't do those things," she said through bitter tears. "I couldn't move on. All this time, I've been in love with you."

"The last time you looked at me, you thought I was a mad man." He climbed to his feet and turned his back to her, facing the fire.

"But you knew I would one day discover the truth," she pointed out. "You said so, yourself."

"And, by then, I'd expected that you would have moved on."

She shook her head as tears continued to fall down her cheeks. "It wasn't until last year, when I met your younger you—Mariela's groom, that I finally began to bury the hope of being with you again. I understood how you must have felt the day you held Mariela as an infant."

Markos knelt beside her. "My, God, Denise. I'm so sorry. I had no idea. I had no understanding of our closed causal loop until the old woman found me."

"Just promise me that you won't leave me again," she said, "not until…"

"I promise," he said before he covered her lips with his.

CHAPTER TWENTY

The Present

Denise lay in bed beside Markos in the penthouse suite of the downtown Marriott playing all that she had learned over and over in her head. Markos snored softly beside her, unaffected by the dapple of sunlight streaming from the open curtain onto his face.

A realization suddenly hit her, and she sat up in bed.

Markos stirred and asked sleepily, "Are you okay?"

"You have to take me to the other worlds," she said. "I need to learn about them and map them out. I need to convince your *younger you* to go back in time *before* you disappear, while I still have my memories, so I can show him what to do."

He turned on his side to face her and stroked her bare shoulder. "Calm down and listen to me, okay?"

She took a deep breath and nodded.

"We have three years together before I'm gone. Do you really want to spend your time mapping the other worlds and searching for a way to change the past or the future? Or do you want to live in the present, for once, with me?"

He was right. The two of them had wasted their whole lives trying to change the past and the future. Neither of them had ever lived happily in the present—except for the moment they had together on the upper deck of *The Mariela* in March 2018. In the twenty years that they'd known one another, that was the only moment in their lives when they were each fully present.

"I want to be with you, Markos," she said. "I want to relish every moment we have together."

He propped himself on an elbow and leaned over her. Gazing into her eyes, he smoothed her hair from her face and caressed her cheek. "We will always have these moments, even if you don't remember them, okay?"

She smiled up at him. "I guess I'll have to become a seer so I can experience all time at once."

Markos narrowed his eyes and then widened them as he sat up.

"What is it?" She sat up beside him, putting a hand on his back.

"It was you," he said. "The old woman who spoke to me on Sector 200. I can't believe it didn't occur to me. It was you."

She covered her mouth as she pieced what he was saying together. "That means that one day, I'll find a way to experience all time at once. I won't forget you, and you'll always exist with me."

"For now, let's have some fun."

He leaned over and kissed her neck, sending chills of pleasure across her skin. She laid back on her pillow, cherishing the thrill of his lips on her earlobe, her chin, her mouth. Then he slid his lips to her throat, to her bare breasts, making her nipples taut. His tongue danced on each nipple, before he moved down to her abdomen, to her belly button, and lower. She gasped as he showed her how amazing, how wonderful, living in this moment would be.

Denise couldn't stop herself from mapping out the sectors of the parallel worlds that Markos and she visited together, but she didn't allow it to become an ambition that consumed her. They took his private jet, *The Denise*, back to his home on Sector 98. She enjoyed learning about the other worlds and the sometimes subtle and sometimes extreme differences to their world as she encountered them. But mostly, she enjoyed spending every day and night with her one true love.

She kept her Houston apartment and continued her work at NASA, but, due to her travels, she became a consultant rather than a full-time employee. She also made sure to visit her family once a month, where she enjoyed cooking for them and baking her famous lemon cream cake. She went without Markos to those visits, knowing her family couldn't fathom who he was. And she fostered a mentor-like relationship with her niece's Markos, who wanted to learn how to cook from her, among other things. So, when she wasn't with *her* Markos, she was with the other.

Three years went by much too quickly, but Denise kept reminding herself that one day, she would learn how to experience all time, and she would return to these precious moments, these amazing moments that gave her life meaning. She focused on the present, lived in the here and now, and tried not to worry about yesterday or tomorrow.

But she knew the day was fast approaching when Markos would no longer be with her, and in the last few months of that third year, she found it difficult to feel joy.

On their last night together, they lay in bed in her Houston apartment, clinging to one another. She wept so much that she expected to eventually run out of tears. Markos stroked her hair, her cheek, her arm. He made love to her and reminded her again and again that they would exist together in the closed causal loop for all eternity, and that one day in her future, she would see it—she would see all time at once.

She didn't want to sleep that night, but at some point, she must have fallen, because, the next thing she knew, she was opening her eyes to the sunshine streaming in through her half-open blinds. She reached her arm out to touch Markos but found the bed beside her empty.

She sat up, full of panic, gripping the sheets. "Markos! Markos!"

"I'm right here," he said from where he was standing across the room in his robe, with a cup of coffee.

He sat the coffee on the dresser and smiled at her. "I've been watching you sleep."

She climbed out of bed and went to him. "I thought…"

"I know." He kissed her cheek, her chin, her mouth. "But I'm still here."

"I love you, Markos. I'll always love you."

She wrapped her arms around his neck, relishing the feel of his arms holding her waist and pressing her close against him.

"I'll always love you, Denise."

They stood together near the window, holding each other for many minutes when something began to feel different. Denise felt dizzy for a moment and looked at her reflection in the mirror. She supposed Mariela's diagnosis had kept her from a good night's sleep. She shuffled to her kitchen and made herself a pot of coffee. Then an idea hit her: She would find a way to bend back space-time so she could get Mariela's cancer discovered early enough to be successfully treated.

She ran to her phone, where it was charging on her bedside table, and called Markos.

"Can you meet for lunch today?" she said quickly. "I think I figured out a way to save Mariela!"

Denise spent the next several months utilizing the interdimensional submarine her team designed and built at NASA on several voyages with Markos. They tried the Artic Sea, but ice bergs proved too great a threat. Settling on the Mariana Trench, they took the sub and her tachyonic cannon to see if her years of work on closed time-like curves and interdimensional travel was possible. Mariela's impending death had become the impetus to speeding up the realization of Denise's life's work.

She could tell the young Markos was nervous as he climbed into the tiny cockpit with her.

"Are you sure this isn't just an elaborate coffin you've built for us?" he asked her.

She laughed. "I promise that I wouldn't put you in any real danger. If any of our systems fail, I'll abort the dive and take us back to the yacht, okay?"

He nodded as he clung to his shoulder harness.

She flipped on the engines as the pressure chamber in the hull of the ship filled with water.

"Adventure awaits," she said to him with a smile.

THE END

Thank you for reading my story. If you enjoyed it, please consider leaving a review. Reviews help other readers to find my books, which helps me.

Please enjoy this excerpt from another dark thriller romance from *The Nightmare Collection*, *The Mystery Tomb*.

CHAPTER ONE

The Mësingw

Samantha Beck stood, hunched over a screen, sifting through bones and dirt.

Her associate, Mark Farms, was bent over the screen across from her, photographing a scrap of leather with a digital camera. The two-by-four-foot wire-meshed screen lay atop two wooden sawhorses. Several of these were set up around their excavation site.

Samantha took off her dirty gloves and held up a sherd of pottery in the Pennsylvania summer sun. So far, two weeks on the site had turned up nothing. She doubted she'd be able to convince her professor to trust her again, so this might be her last chance to prove that her grandmother was a Lenape descendant. The landowner wouldn't let them stay indefinitely, and O'Neil, their department head, was sure to pull the plug any day now.

"Algonquian markings." She pointed to marks at the base of the sherd where an upward turned bow preceded a series of rectangular engravings, and her chest bloomed with hope. "I've seen these on Lenape pipes in Oklahoma. And here's another turtle. I still don't know what that signifies." She brought down the sherd and continued sifting through the screen, vaguely aware that the sun was going down.

"Look at this scrap of leather," Mark said.

"Is that the one the baby was wrapped in?"

Mark nodded. "But something's not right about this site. I agree with you. It's like they were moved." He took another photo.

Professor Ricardo Gomez's cell phone rang out across the excavation site.

Mark glanced over at the professor, who fumbled in the pocket of his blue jeans with his one free hand for his cell phone. "Maybe the professor can shed some light on this."

"The bodies *must* have been moved after burial, after decomposition," she said. "Like, in recent years."

But who would move the bodies, and why?

"Hello?" the professor said into his phone.

Mark shook his head. "You think he'll be on the phone an hour again?"

"The last call wasn't that long."

"We might have time for a quickie."

Comments like that made her wish she wasn't sleeping with him. "If these bodies were moved from their original resting place," she said, ignoring his comment, "I want to know why."

"Give us another four or five days," the professor said into the phone. "It's only been two weeks. No, but there's plenty of evidence to suggest…No. Yes, sir." He turned off the cell phone and stuffed it back into his pocket. "Bastard."

"What's wrong, Professor?" Samantha called to him from across the site.

The short, bony man walked around the excavation units in the ground toward his two graduate students, the brim of his straw hat waving in the wind, making him look like an old scarecrow. "Never mind that now. I think I've found what we're looking for."

Her mouth dropped open.

The professor held a small bandolier bag with its wide, beaded shoulder strap hanging like fully cooked lasagna noodles, its colors of orange and red and turquoise shining from beneath layers of dirt. She had never seen an artifact so perfectly preserved, so well intact.

The professor handed it over to her, and she took it in trembling hands.

"This bag is just like my grandmother's," Samantha whispered, her heart pumping.

"It gets better," the professor said.

Before he could explain further, a black pickup truck skidded onto their site from the dirt road. The driver's window lowered, revealing a man with long black hair and fierce black eyes.

"You guys need to clear on out of here!" He pointed to the tents and the screens nesting in the pasture at the edge of the site. "Get all this stuff out of here! Any arrangements you've made with my grandfather have been cancelled!"

"Who in God's name is this clown?" the professor muttered as Samantha gently laid the artifact on the screen.

Samantha followed the professor toward the truck. "Who are you?"

He gave her a once over and narrowed his eyes. "I should ask the same of you. My grandfather had no right."

"Just fucking great," the professor said.

Samantha gasped. "Do you even realize what we've discovered?"

"This is sacred ground, and those are my people! This isn't open for discussion."

Samantha's face flushed. If he was a descendant, then…

"Your people?" The professor moved nearer to the stranger. "Son, are you saying these bones belonged to your family?"

Samantha held her breath.

"You need to get the hell of my property!" the stranger shouted before driving off.

Descendant or not, Sam wanted to kill him.

"What in the hell was that all about?" Mark said.

"Let's not worry about him right now." The professor returned to the screen and lifted the bandolier bag up like a newborn baby.

Samantha watched as he reversed the inside lining.

"Oh God," the professor said beneath his breath.

"What?" Mark bent over to look at the artifact.

As they leaned over him, he whispered, "The seal."

"The Mësingw?" Mark raised his brows at Samantha.

"Really? Please don't joke with me." Samantha looked more closely at the beads on the lining. Beneath the folds of dirt, she could make out the half red and half black face: The Mësingw.

Her mouth fell open as Mark laughed out loud and patted her on the back. The professor met her eyes, and the two of them smiled before also breaking out into joyous laughter. Then she jumped up in the air, hugging herself. Mark ran a victory lap past the excavation units and all around the site, and she quickly followed, singing "Woohooo!" repeatedly as the sun continued to sink beyond the rolling hills.

"We've done it!" The professor shouted in the evening air.

"We've done it!" Samantha cried, too, returning to the professor, Mark not far behind.

She sank on the ground and covered her face with her hands. It had been such a long journey, and she had nearly given up. Tears sprang to her eyes. Her grandmother had been right: Their family was descended from a tribe that had branched away from the Lenape.

"The lost tribe," the professor said, tears streaming from his eyes. "My word, Samantha, you were right. My word, woman, you've discovered the lost tribe of Unikwëti!"

Samantha left the bathroom on the second floor of Gellermann Manor and danced in her robe toward what had been her room for the past two weeks. She couldn't believe four years of research had finally paid off. Her grandmother would be so pleased to know there was a way to join the modern tribe. And the professor would have to get tenure after this. And what about her? Surely this would get her a job just about anywhere, or at least somewhere good. She was so tired of living off her parents and eager to pay them back for all their generosity. At twenty-five years of age and still living with her parents, her days of feeling like a loser were over.

She hummed to the song playing on her iPod until, as she neared her door, the stranger from earlier appeared at the top of the stairs across from her. She'd had this part of the house to herself for two weeks, so it was a shock to see someone this evening. Her face flushed as she clutched her robe and pulled the tiny ear buds from her ears.

His long dark hair was wet like hers.

"Just great," he said.

She opened her mouth to speak, but nothing came out.

"You and the others are staying *here*?" He looked her up and down.

"Are you?"

He took a step closer to her. "I live here."

She backed up toward the door of her room. "Listen. Please don't make us…"

"I come all the way home from Iraq to find *this*."

"We've finally found the tribal seal on a bandolier bag that's just like my…"

He took a step closer, his face inches from hers. "You better start packing."

For a moment she thought he was going to kiss her. She stammered back and said, "Look, I'll just go get dressed." She entered her room, breathless, and closed the door.

Everyone else was already seated at the table when Samantha arrived at seven sharp. Brandon Gellermann wore a formal suit, as he had every evening since they'd been there.

He stood up when she entered. "Good evening, Samantha."

"Good evening. I hope I haven't kept everyone waiting." She took her seat beside him across from Mark and the professor.

The table was clothed with ivory silk trimmed with Chantilly lace. Samantha noticed a new setting tonight. Royal Crown Derby, Ashby pattern. China was her mother's love, after her family. Their home was full of collections from all over the world. Samantha turned her plate over. The maker's mark was green, indicating World War II production. This meant each of the pink flowers was painted by hand. Brandon had a valuable collection.

"Not at all." Brandon took his seat. "We're all just a little on edge tonight. I was just telling the professor that I wasn't expecting my grandson home for another month."

For the first time in two weeks, a fifth place had been set on the table next to her.

"Will he be joining us?" she asked, dreading the answer.

"Unfortunately, no," Brandon said. "Charles has been in Afghanistan for nearly six months, and tonight he wasn't up to company."

Relieved, Samantha twisted the napkin in her lap beneath the well-dressed dinner table as the butler entered with plates of salad. As she picked up her fork, Sam said to Brandon, "Your grandson didn't seem too pleased to see us."

Mark laughed. "That's an understatement."

Nodding, Brandon said, "Yes. He told me his feelings about the matter. I must say I never expected him to oppose your research."

"What does this mean?" Samantha asked, taking a sip of her water. "Do we really have to clear out?"

"I was just telling your professor that you may continue your excavation as long as you wish, but this is the difference: I want you to leave everything you find here with me."

"What?" the professor asked, with a touch of indignation.

"You may photograph as much as you'd like," Brandon said. "But I'm afraid that everything you find belongs to my grandson, for he is, er, a descendant of the bodies you have discovered."

"How do you know?" Mark asked.

"Charles's father was Indian, er, Native American. He died when Charles was eight years old. There used to be a large group of them living here."

"Here, on your property?" the professor asked.

Brandon nodded.

"Did you personally know and interact with them?" Samantha asked.

"Unfortunately, yes," Brandon said, his face turning red. And before anyone could ask more, he added, "Anyway, those bones are his ancestors, and the relics are his, too. And he doesn't wish for any of your findings to be removed from this property. In return, I'll reimburse the sum you paid to me for the use of my land. Every dime. Does that sound fair enough?"

"Hold on just a minute." Samantha brushed a strand of her long brown hair from her face. "First of all, your grandson is not the only living descendant of that tribe, and I can prove it. And second of all, you signed a contract agreeing to donate our most important findings to the university."

"Oh, dear," Brandon said. He turned to the professor. "Surely you understand my change of heart?"

The professor frowned. "Why did you agree to let us have the artifacts in the first place?"

"I didn't expect Charles to return from Iraq so soon," Brandon said. "I honestly had hoped…but now that he knows, my hands are tied."

"We have a contract," Samantha said again.

"I suppose I'll have to ask my attorney to sort out this matter."

"Does this mean you want us to leave?" Mark asked.

"Hmm. I'll speak to my attorney in the morning. Hopefully after breakfast, I'll have something to tell you."

After dinner, Brandon invited them all for cocktails in his study, as he had done each night, but only the professor accepted. Samantha was frustrated and not in the mood for company. As she and Mark left the dining room together and entered the foyer, where the winding staircase stretched up the expanse of the three floors of the manor, she said, "I think I'll go for a walk."

"Just imagine what Gellermann's grandson might be able to tell us about that tribe." Mark glanced up at the exquisite crystal chandelier, which sparkled like diamonds. "Brandon said Charles was eight when his father died. He may have learned some things about his people the tribes in Oklahoma and Canada can't tell us. Man, if only he would cooperate. It's a damn shame."

"I wonder if there are others, besides Charles."

Mark shrugged. "Seems likely." Then he added, "You might not realize this, but under most state statutes, the archaeological team has to get written permission from any known descendants of a burial site. Even though the Lebanon County Historical Society told us they didn't know of any, Gellermann's grandson might still have a case."

"Well, maybe he'll come around to our way of seeing things before we get into litigation. You never know."

"The eternal optimist, ladies and gentlemen." He grinned.

She gave him a smile.

"By the way, you look great tonight," he said. "Really sexy in that black dress with your hair down."

"Thanks." She scanned his wavy blond hair, handsome blue eyes, and tanned skin. "You look nice, too."

"Do you mind if I walk with you?"

Leave the guy alone, she admonished herself. She knew she shouldn't keep sleeping with him. The liberties he took with her because of it were too annoying. And she didn't want to hurt him. "I think I need some alone time. So much has happened today, I haven't even digested it all."

"Yeah, I know what you mean. I guess I could use some alone time myself now that you mention it." He kissed her cheek and patted her behind. "Good night."

Another reason to stop sleeping with him. She forced a smile. "Good night."

After he had taken a few steps up the stairs, he turned back to her and asked, "So what's 'petit mal,' anyway? Sounds familiar, but I'm not sure what it means."

She had been talking about her childhood seizures with him earlier.

"Petit mal seizures look like staring spells. An electrical storm would go off in my brain."

"No kidding?"

"Really. And it would last up to thirty seconds at a time."

"Would you fall down?"

She smiled and shook her head. "No. Nothing like that. I could stand and even walk. I just couldn't hear or see anything clearly."

"Damn. Not too fun."

"No. My teachers used to think I wasn't paying attention. Once I started taking medication—the right medication—everything changed. Now the doctor thinks I've outgrown epilepsy. I haven't been on meds for years."

"That's great."

"I brought it up earlier because you shouldn't be so hard on your nephew. I mean, what you were describing—the problems he's having at school and at home—actually sound familiar. It might not be his fault." They'd had a lot of time on the site to talk these past two weeks.

He smiled down at her and then continued up the stairs. "Thanks."

As Samantha walked through the foyer, she overheard part of the conversation between the professor and Brandon. She stood inside the doorway, on the verge of joining them now that she was rid of Mark.

"Excuse me for being so bold, Brandon," the professor said, both of them apparently comfortable with their coffee and cigars, each in over-stuffed chairs on either side of an empty fireplace at the back of the room, and unaware of her presence.

Above the mantel behind them loomed a huge elk head, its glassy eyes watching over them. Samantha shuddered.

Brandon raised his eyebrows and waited expectantly for the professor's question, exhaling a stream of smoke that swirled up toward the ceiling. "What is it?"

"Well, I couldn't help but notice these past two weeks that you hold a strong emotion, something like contempt, in regard to the Native American people who once lived on your land. Am I wrong?"

Brandon avoided the professor's eyes. "No, Ricardo. Your observation is correct."

Samantha moved out of sight, not wanting to interrupt, and anxious to hear the old man's reply.

"I'm sorry. It's none of my business."

"I didn't always hate them. They were well liked by my family for over two centuries. I liked them, too. My wife and I both did until something terrible happened. Oh, dear. Forgive me if I don't go into details. It's too disturbing."

"Of course. I understand. I apologize for bringing it up. Let's talk instead about how you came to own that beautiful bronze of Beethoven in your foyer."

"Now that I would be pleased to divulge."

Samantha crept away from the study through the foyer toward the front double oak doors. What had happened between Brandon Gellermann and her ancestors that made him hate them all these years? She walked around to the back of the estate and down a steep hill to the small creek below. Steppingstones made the trek easier for her, and as soon as she neared the creek and was out of the light thrown off by the exterior fixtures around the manor, she pulled off her black pumps and carried them as she walked along the water to a large rock beside a tree. The thick trunk of the tree leaned over the running creek nearly parallel with the surface, and from the rock beside it, Samantha could sit and hold onto the trunk for balance as she moved her dangling legs through the cool water.

Two weeks ago, during a brief tour of the manor, Brandon had told her the name of the creek—Lethe, which was also the name of the river of forgetfulness in the Greek mythological Underworld. She had inwardly laughed at the irony given that she had come to be sure the Unikweti would never be forgotten.

Off in the distance, up the creek to her right, the hills seemed to roll up into darkness, to the end of the earth. The slight breeze over the water refreshed her in spite of the troubling turn of events.

She wriggled her toes in the water. The last thing she wanted to think about were her seizures, but Mark's questions made her recall her fourth grade teacher, plump and pear-shaped with gray curly hair swept up in a bun. She wore a red pantsuit that was too small, the buttons of her jacket threatening to pop, like her temper. She stooped over Samantha's desk. "Samantha, have you been listening?"

"Yes, Mrs. Bradley."

"Then tell me what I just said."

"If an object has more protons than electrons, it has a positive charge."

Several of the children had giggled.

"That's what I said a minute ago. I want you to repeat what I said last, just now. Who can say what I've just said to the rest of the class?"

All but Samantha raised their hands.

Mrs. Bradley put her stiff, cruel face to Samantha's ear. "Pay attention this time," she rasped. Mrs. Bradley stood upright, tugged at her tight red jacket, and called on the boy three chairs behind Samantha.

"Yes, Jack?"

"We measure the strength of an electrical current in amps."

"Got that, girl?" Mrs. Bradley spat, narrowing her cold eyes.

Samantha had nodded, fighting back tears. "Yes, Mrs. Bradley."

Samantha stared at Lethe Creek, wishing some things could be forgotten.

"Beck, that you?" a voice came from out of the darkness.

She straightened her back, pulled her legs together, and looked in the direction of the voice.

"Charles?" she whispered, unable to see the figure on the rocks behind the leaning tree.

"Not Charles. Tukihëla Nisha."

"But your grandfather said…"

"He's not too fond of my Native American side."

Somewhat frightened by the angry tone in his voice, Samantha glanced back at the well-lit manor on the hill and then back at the dark figure behind the leaning tree.

She climbed to her feet. "I didn't mean to offend you. I didn't know."

He took five steps toward her and stood in her view with the tree between their feet. He would only have to step over the tree to be next to her. The moon was behind him, and his face was in shadows. Samantha could not read its expression. She took another step back.

"I didn't hear you come down here," she said. "What do you want?"

"I want you to answer my question. Why can't you let them be? Why do you have to disturb and humiliate my ancestors like this?"

"I don't want to humiliate them," she insisted.

"You want to display their bones and their goods like animals in a zoo." He stepped over the tree and stood inches from her, bringing the fear back to her trembling body, but his voice became gentler. "How can someone so beautiful be so heartless?"

Did he say beautiful?

Hang on. Did he say heartless? No one had ever called her heartless.

She backed away, gathered her shoes from the rock, and hurried a few steps up the hill from him before turning to say, "You're the heartless one. I want to give those people a voice. You want to stifle their contribution to modern society before they even have a chance to make it."

She reached around her face and bunched her windblown hair in a single fist. "Well, I won't let you do it." Then she turned and walked away, back up the hill to the distant manor.

Back in her room, Samantha changed into her comfortable nightshirt, grabbed her cell phone, and climbed into bed. How dare he, she thought. How dare he try to stop her from learning about her people?

The silver-framed photograph on the antique nightstand fell back, so she set it upright.

She realized now, upon closer inspection, that this was a picture of Tukihëla's mother, Rebecca. Brandon had shown her another portrait down in the music room. This photo was taken when she was a girl of ten or so. Two barrettes pinned back blonde curls, and grey eyes narrowed in a scowl. Rebecca lifted her little chin defiantly as she stood in her plaid dress in the front of Gellermann Manor holding a red dachshund. Samantha put the photo back on the nightstand beneath the antique Tiffany lamp and sat against her pillows on the bed.

Samantha sighed in the full-sized antique oak poster bed and sank into the cream satin linen, as she stared at the enormous window opening on to the front of the estate. She turned off the Tiffany lamp so she could gaze out the window and the starry landscape and forget the man who called himself Tukihëla Nisha.

She decided to look up his name in her Algonquian dictionary, so she flipped back on the lamp and grabbed the book from her bag.

Tukihëla meant "awaken." She leafed through to the N's. Nisha meant "two."

She slammed shut the book and returned it to her bag on the floor by her bed. She flipped off the lamp, closed her eyes, and pleaded with the river of forgetfulness. Why couldn't she get the image of Tukihëla Nisha out of her head?

When the image refused to leave, she took up the cell phone and called her grandma to tell her the news of the day's discovery. She was going to wait until morning, but then remembered it was still only seven o'clock in Texas.

Plus, her grandma's voice would cheer her up.

"So those skeletons you found are without question ancestors of mine?"

"I believe so, Grandma. I'm ninety-nine percent sure they are. We haven't gotten the DNA test yet. I've sent samples of my blood and fibers from several of the bones to our lab."

"You should use my blood, or your father's."

"What does it matter?"

"You're right. Of course, it doesn't matter. Anyway, I'll have to come up and see the place for myself!"

"Not right now, though I'd absolutely love that. There's a bit of a kink in our plans. Another descendant has appeared, and he doesn't like what we're doing."

"Oh, dear. That's too bad. I hope you won't let this obtuse person stop you."

"You know me."

"That's right. So I won't come now, but I will come eventually."

"I'd like that."

"A fellow descendant? I really must meet him."

Samantha imagined her boisterous grandmother meeting the solemn Tukihëla Nisha.

"By the way, it was our discovery of the Mësingw that provided the final proof," Samantha added.

"You mean Misink, don't you?"

"Isn't that what I said?"

"No. I've told you before, you need to say 'sink,' like a kitchen sink."

"Grandma, I know what I'm talking about. I interviewed lots of folks in Oklahoma. They even spelled it for me."

"M-I-S-I-N-K. Short for Misinkhalikàn."

"That's not what they said. Oh, it doesn't matter, anyway. It's the same guy, I'm sure of it, with the face that's half red and…"

"Half black. Look, I know what I'm talking about, too. My Grandma Kexi told me a story about Misink. I told it to you when you were little, but your mother didn't like it. She was afraid my stories would undermine your Christian values."

"But you're Christian."

"I know, I know. Well, we both know your mother can be a bit ridiculous. Anyway, shall I tell you the story again?"

"Absolutely."

"Alright then. A long, long time ago there lived three boys no one loved, not even their parents. People threw rocks at them and called them names, and no one knows why. One day when they were out in the woods, a hairy-looking person with a face painted half red and half black jumped in front of them and said he was Misinkhalikàn. He said he would protect them from the others. So, they followed him to the sky, and he showed them his home, promising them strength and power.

"Years later, after they had been accepted by their tribe and had become leaders, they would often hear Misink's peculiar call, 'Ho-ho-ho!' and they would follow the sound to the middle of the woods where that great hairy person would be herding the deer."

Samantha interrupted. "Ho-ho-ho? Like Santa Clause?"

"Exactly."

Samantha shifted on the bed and pulled back the duvet to slide beneath the covers and listen more comfortably. She lay down on the pillow. "Go on, Grandma."

"Anyway, about this time, for some unknown reason, the Unikwëti had stopped their bi-annual worship ceremonies. Ten years went by without a single tribute to the spirits. Then a great earthquake came upon their land and lasted for twelve moons. They built a new long house of bark and worshipped all winter, praying for help.

"In the spring, they heard the peculiar cry of Misink through the forest, 'Ho-ho-ho!' The three men who had once befriended him followed his sound and met with him in the forest, where he gave them instructions for a new ceremony to ensure their safety from earthquakes and other doom.

"Misink told them they must create a mask using paint, half black and half red like his face, and he would put his power into the mask so whoever would wear it, Misink would be there among the people. The man must carry a turtle-shell rattle, a bandolier bag, and a staff. Misink told them he would keep the deer close by if they would pay homage to him through this ceremony at least once a year."

"How cool. So did they? Did our people pay homage?"

"Yes. Twice a year. Once in the fall and once in the spring. Grandma Kexi told me Misink comes to warn humans when we are not living in harmony with the other creatures and with Mother Earth."

"What a great story, Grandma."

"You remember years ago—I can't remember—when all that talk came out about Bigfoot?"

"That was before my time, but I know what you're talking about."

"I remember wondering to myself if it wasn't Misink whose footprints were left behind and whose big hairy body was caught on tape. Maybe he'd come to protest cruelty to animals—you know, testing on them needlessly and such."

Samantha laughed. "Who knows, right?"

"It just might have been Misink!"

<u>CHAPTER TWO</u>

Rebecca

Rebecca slid the eight-foot aluminum boat from the bank of the creek, hopped in with a bucket of live perch she had caught that morning, and paddled up the creek toward her drop lines.

She couldn't believe Daddy was going to send her to Hartridge after all. She didn't want to go away to boarding school. She wanted to stay here where she could run her lines every day and play with Sandra and Nancy up in her tree house when they came to visit their grandparents in the spring.

The hot summer sun had yielded to a cool evening breeze, and Rebecca now wished she had worn long sleeves. The small pool of water that had leaked into the bottom of the boat soaked into her shoes and socks and chilled her.

Daddy had said she needed to learn how to become a smart and proper young lady. Hadn't she become one already?

I know more than most ten-year-olds.

She eyed the first drop line—a bit of twine tied to a willow near the bank of the creek. At the end of the twine was a shad stripped on a straight hook and probably a nice catfish by the way the twine was moving in circles. She paddled toward the willow.

What's more useful, playing piano and doing embroidery or catching dinner?

Her father used to set and run the lines with her, but a year ago he had broken his hip in a skiing accident, and though he had undergone a hip replacement, he wasn't comfortable paddling in their little boat.

He'd fish with her from the bank with rod and reels when they wanted perch, but she now set and ran the drop lines herself.

She heard a rustling in the nearby brush and looked up as she approached the willow. She didn't see anything.

That sounded bigger than a squirrel. Could it be a deer? A raccoon?

She grabbed the willow and flung the rope that was tied to her boat around a branch to keep the boat from drifting while she checked her line. She heard the rustling again and looked up.

When the rustling stopped and she still didn't see anything moving along the brush, she pulled the catfish into the boat.

"Far-out! That's a four-pounder for sure!" she cried.

She waited for the flapping fish to settle down. Then she pinched the shaft of the straight hook with needle-nose pliers and grabbed the catfish beneath its poisonous fins with her other hand, leaning her weight on the fish to keep it still. Then she broke the tip of each of the three fins, removed the hook from its mouth, laid the fish in the bottom of the boat, and baited the hook with one of the perch from her bucket.

"You're the biggest I've caught in a while," Rebecca said to the catfish, tossing the line with its wiggling perch back into the water.

The fish lay at her feet, worn out and gasping.

As she paddled up the creek toward her next line, she heard rustling along the bank again. She paddled so she wouldn't drift back, but she kept her eyes on the bank.

She found nothing on her second and third lines, so she quickly baited and moved up the creek to her fourth, which she could see had something pulling on the end of it.

As she flung her rope around the branch of a tree and tied on, she heard the rustling again, and this time, when she looked up toward the bank, a strange painted face stared down at her. Half of the face was red and the other black. Bearskin draped around the figure's shoulders.

She screamed and toppled back, nearly falling from the boat.

Quickly, she untied the rope from her boat and tossed it overboard. She snatched her paddle and used it to push from the tree, allowing herself to drift downstream. Then she paddled away, catching glances of what she now realized was just a man, but a scary man, nonetheless, running along the bank, following her.

When she reached the place where she had docked, at the rock by the leaning tree, she heard Zugi barking on the bank at the painted man.

"Good girl!" Rebecca yelled. "Get him, girl!"

Although Zugi's red, hot-dog-shaped body was not all that threatening, the barking accomplished what Rebecca had hoped: Daddy was bearing down the hill from the back porch, calling to her.

"Rebecca? Everything okay down here? Zugi? What's the matter, girl?"

The painted man disappeared.

"You look adorable," Rebecca's mother told her as they stood together before the mirror in Rebecca's dressing room.

Rebecca didn't like the stiff material of her plaid school uniform. She rather liked the knee-high socks and new shoes, but the dress smelled funny and felt itchy.

"Now let's pin back your hair, so we can see your pretty face."

Rebecca flinched from her mother. "No. I don't want barrettes."

"But you won't be able to see." The mop of golden curls fell into Rebecca's eyes.

"I can see."

Her mother put her hands on her hips and sighed.

Rebecca didn't mean to make her mother angry. She wanted to hug her and tell her how much she would miss her and please, please don't make her go away to school!

"I'm asking you to wear these barrettes for your own good. Now please do as I say. You exasperate me."

Tears streamed down Rebecca's cheeks. "Yes, Mama."

"Quit crying like a baby over these silly barrettes."

Rebecca pushed her mother's hands away from her hair. "I'm not a baby!"

"I didn't say you were a baby. I said to quit acting like one."

"I'm not a baby! I'm not even going to miss you when I'm gone! The only one who loves me in this whole wide world is Zugi!" Rebecca ran from the room calling for her dog.

"Zugi? Where are you, girl?"

"Rebecca! Come back here!"

Rebecca ran from the house.

"Zugi?"

She followed the steppingstones down to the creek where she heard Zugi barking.

"What's the matter, girl?" Rebecca stayed back, afraid she would find the painted man she had seen a few days ago. She had told Daddy about him, and he had said not to go to the creek without him. "Zugi!" she called from the side of the hill. "Come here!"

Then Rebecca heard music coming from the creek. A single instrument, maybe a flute, sounded from the trees.

Zugi stopped barking.

"Zugi?"

She crept a little further down the hill toward the creek and the melody lifting up from the trees and into the wind and sky.

"Hello? Who's there?"

The music stopped, and a teenage boy jumped from the oak tree in front of her with a flute of wood in his hand and said, "Me. Attie."

Rebecca thought he must be at least sixteen, much too old a boy to be talking to her, but she asked, "Are you the painted man?"

"Misink? You saw Misink?" and with that, he ran up the hill and into the woods.

Rebecca had seen the Indians many times, but never had she seen them so close to her house. And never before this week had she seen the painted man whom even the Indians apparently feared.

Moments later, Rebecca's mother hastened down the hill. "You come to me when I call you, young lady!"

Instead of running away, Rebecca charged up the hill and flung herself against her mother, wrapping her arms around her waist and sobbing uncontrollably.

"Don't let Daddy make me go. I want to stay here!"

"Now, now." Her mother plopped onto the grass in her soft, flared pants and pulled Rebecca onto her lap. "That's enough crying." She smoothed the curls away from her daughter's face and kissed her cheeks several times. "You know Mama and Daddy love you, don't you?"

Rebecca nodded, clutching Zugi as the dachshund added herself to their bundle on the grass.

"Daddy and I want you to go to Hartridge so you'll be able to get in to the best universities. We want you to have all the best chances for success. We want you to have choices when you're older, so you can be happy doing what you want to do."

"But I'm happy here."

Her mother kissed her again and gave her another hug. "We'll visit weekends, and you'll come home for Christmas and summers. Just give it a chance, will you?"

Rebecca shrugged. "What choice do I have?"

Her mother pulled them up to their feet, patted her daughter and Zugi, and said, "Now let's go take that photograph, shall we? I want to remember the day my little girl started becoming a young woman."

Rebecca held her mother's hand as they walked up the hill.

"Will you wear the barrettes for me?" her mother asked.

Rebecca groaned. "Okay, Mama."

EVA POHLER

Eva Pohler is a *USA Today* bestselling author of over thirty novels in multiple genres, including mysteries, thrillers, and young adult paranormal romance based on Greek mythology. Her books have been described as "addictive" and "sure to thrill"—*Kirkus Reviews*.

To learn more about Eva and her books, and to sign up to hear about new releases, and sales, please visit her website at www.evapohler.com.

9 781958 390566